New

"I'd kill you this second if I could,"

★

Stone managed to mutter, through lips that felt puffy.

"Brave words from a man who can't move a muscle," Patton laughed, turning to the others who joined in. Stone looked down for the first time and saw what he was tied to. He was standing, raised up on an X-shaped wooden structure, hands and feet stretched apart and chained to the four ends of the archaic device.

"We found this," Patton said, reaching out and tapping the wood just below Stone's outstretched arm. "It came from a museum and was once used for precisely the purpose we're going to put it to tonight." He looked at Stone expectantly. And sure enough the imprisoned man had to bite.

"And what purpose is that?"

"Torture, obviously," the General replied, sweeping his hands around the aluminum framed hut. "In fact, I had this place constructed just for you. Because I knew we'd meet again. And that was all I wanted."

He reached f   Stone's head slamr
wood...

ALSO BY CRAIG SARGENT

The Last Ranger
The Savage Stronghold
The Madman's Mansion
The Rabid Brigadier
The Warlord's Revenge*

Published by
POPULAR LIBRARY   *forthcoming

THE WAR WEAPONS

CRAIG SARGENT

POPULAR LIBRARY

An Imprint of Warner Books, Inc.

A Warner Communications Company

POPULAR LIBRARY EDITION

Popular Library® and the fanciful P design are registered
trademarks of Warner Books, Inc.

Cover design by Rolf Erickson
Cover illustration by Norm Eastman

Popular Library books are published by
Warner Books, Inc.
666 Fifth Avenue
New York, N.Y. 10103

 A Warner Communications Company

Printed in the United States of America

First Printing: October, 1987

10 9 8 7 6 5 4 3 2 1

CHAPTER

ONE

THE SKELETONS burned like black jewels in the snow-filled air. What was left of their charred ash skin glowed with little red shivers of dancing flame along the outer edges. Most of the flesh on the five bodies had been reduced to a charcoallike material, similar to something found at the bottom of a campfire long after the wood had burned down. These sculptures of ash had been set aflame from a phosphorus bomb that had fallen in their midst. Then they had been human—their screams had attested to that. Now, after the consuming fire had bitten and chewed through all that was flammable on the human body, they were no longer human but just mounds of shimmering ash, a form of carbon that began crumbling in the cold winds that swept across them—blowing the black dust of what had been ears, noses, fingers, cocks, into the dawn air in small swirling jetties of human flotsam and jetsam.

Martin Stone walked past them, a look of profound disgust on his blood-streaked face. It was hard to tell if the dead sons of bitches were friends or enemies, or if the concept even had meaning anymore. Everyone was his enemy as far as he could see. Friends were enemies whom you used for a short while. And then they tried to kill you unless you got them first. It was that simple. He hadn't made up the fucking rules, that was for damned sure. But he knew what they were. And he'd be a fool not to follow them.

There was a sudden crunching sound beneath his boots, and Stone looked down to see that he'd stepped through what had been a head or a chest or some damned thing on another one of the crisp pieces of human popcorn. He yanked his foot out with a jerk and almost jumped backward, revolted by the disintegrating piece of humanity. A whole shitload of dust followed the pull of the leg and the black flakes and particles exploded up in his face as if a dust bomb had gone off. He was suddenly covered in a cloud of the foul black stuff. Stone waved his hands like propellers in front of him as he rushed forward, sneezing and coughing out the particles of the dead. After about twenty feet he seemed to be clear of the corpse storm, so he stopped, went down on one knee, and rested. The entire experience had made him dizzy. He had just had too damned much over the last twenty-four hours. Almost more than a man could bear.

Stone heard a snorting sound behind him and snapped his head up sharply, reaching for the .44 Magnum that hung at his side, holster flap open, ready for quick draw and fire. But all that his eyes beheld was a bedraggled-looking dog, his pitbull Excaliber, all ninety pounds of white-and-brown-hided cannonball sneezing and spitting up a storm as it tried to eject the foul ashes from its nose and mouth. Somehow, though it really wasn't funny at all, the sight made Stone laugh, and once he started laughing, he couldn't stop. His mouth opened and closed and opened again, and sounds came out that seemed like they weren't even his. Stone knew even as he laughed that he wasn't laughing over anything funny—but over all the pain and death around him. 'Cause if he didn't laugh, he'd cry or end it all. And so he laughed and laughed, his lungs heaving, his eyes rimming with tears for minutes until it hurt so bad, he could hardly breathe. Completely breathless, he stopped. The pitbull was now standing about two feet away, resting on its back paws and staring up at the poor boy with a look of utmost concern as if he were thinking his master had finally gone completely bananas. The dog had always been apprehensive that this might happen from the very start. Its last master had been killed, and this one had always seemed a little edgy. So the dog growled softly beneath its breath as if trying to exorcise the demon of laughing sickness that had taken over its numero-uno food supplier.

"Come here, you dumb dog," Stone said at last, drying his eyes with the edge of a blood-soaked strip of material he had tied around his arm where he had taken a bullet in the battle for Fort Bradley only hours before. The wound was still oozing, but the constant flow of blood it had been spouting had dropped to almost nil. "Now I know why I keep you around, you mangy son of a bitch," Stone said. He scratched the bullterrier around the ears and noticed that the thing was absolutely coated with blood and specks of flesh, little wounds and burns; even pieces of twisted shrapnel and twigs covered its coat. "'Cause you make me laugh," Stone continued, "and you're about the only goddamn thing that does in a world that basically doesn't have shit to laugh about. But I'll tell you something else, pal—you need a fucking bath. You look like shit, you know that?" The pitbull whined and got a hangdog kind of expression. Then it raised its head up toward Stone with a skeptical glance, as if to say, "Have you taken a look at yourself lately?"

Stone rose to his feet from his kneeling position and felt a wave of dizziness and nausea sweep through, and he almost buckled over again.

"Come on, come on," he said sharply to himself, gritting his teeth hard. Now wasn't the fucking time to pass out. Not in the middle of a battle zone where the bodies were still smoldering. He raised his head and focused on the flames that rose everywhere around him, rose from what had been Fort Bradley, home of the New American Army, the NAA, until about six o'clock that morning. That was until Martin Stone—accompanied by a force of motorcycle-gang killers, Mafia hitmen, mountain bandits, and general all-around psychotic murderers under his momentary command—had attacked and, from the looks of it, pretty much done in what had been perhaps the largest "military" base in the country —a fortified installation with nearly five hundred men, artillery, helicopters, even a whole parking lot full of tanks. That's what it had been, anyway. But no more. Now secondary explosions still raged like bonfires, and spires of smoke coming from every section of the fort all joined together and rose up through the melting snow to build a dome of orange and red that extended up half a mile into the sky.

It had been one of the hardest decisions Stone had ever made in his life—and he had had to make some damned hard ones lately. The New American Army could have done great things for the surrounding wastelands, for the towns and roads ruled by the cutthroats and slime who now seemed to run things in America. The NAA could have been the first real challenge to the crime lords who ruled it all. Except for one thing—General Patton III, the man who ran it. At first Stone had been taken in by his words, his charm, his vision of an America cleansed of the filth, restored to its former beauty and power. But then Stone had seen deeper into the man's plans, had heard him talk of the "extermination" of certain races and religions. Had heard him speak of the "purification by fire that must occur." And Stone had come to see that the man wasn't a good man but an evil one, perhaps one of the darkest who had ever lived. And incredibly dangerous because he was far smarter than the common crime lords, and because he had that most dangerous of all motivations—a self-righteous cause. And Martin Stone had known that it was possible, very possible, that the general would succeed. Then the world would see the "Pax Pattoni" that would last ten thousand years. A peace of slaves, a peace of the dead.

Stone looked around, spat out another gob of human ash, and started forward, moving very slowly, as his senses were on full alert for some reason. He tried to erase the image of General Patton's eyes staring at him with pure hate. "You're the greatest traitor America has ever known," Patton had said before he had tried to kill Stone. He hadn't succeeded, but Martin Stone had no illusions that that state of affairs was going to last very long. That would-be Führer had escaped and headed toward one of two missile silos under his command. Silos that each contained a ten-megaton missile. Patton had vowed to take Stone out if it was the last thing he ever did. And if Stone knew one thing about the general, it was that he kept his word. Stone glanced up and tried to see through the thick snow that just kept dropping from the skies as if all the tears of the dead had crystallized and an endless stream of them had waterfalled down. But it was too thick to penetrate, at least for his eyes. Yet in his tightening guts, somehow he could feel his location being fed into a computer, could feel a missile's electronic brain digesting just who it was supposed to annihilate into the tiniest of glowing atoms.

Stone wasn't even sure what the hell it was he was looking for as he moved forward, stepping over debris, as vehicles burned on all sides of him. Perhaps a clue as to just where the hell the general had fled. There was still sporadic fighting going on here and there in the distance, though clearly the bulk of it was over. His only hope was that Patton had left some indication as to just where the other missile silos were. Stone knew that there were at least two, possibly three of the still functioning underground launchpads somewhere in Colorado and Utah. The asshole would take out the whole damned state if he launched. Talk about overkill——

Patton was ready to destroy some of the most beautiful forests, lakes, and rivers that were left in the whole country just to get one man—him. Stone wondered if he'd hurt the fellow's feelings just a little.

But just who was going to get the privilege of killing Martin Stone suddenly became an immediate concern as Stone heard a crunching sound to his left and turned to see more of the blistered corpses. Only these seemed to be moving, their black bodies shivering and crumbling as they rose. As Stone stood frozen in stark terror, the filth-coated things seemed to rise right up off the ground and come toward him. Suddenly he saw human flesh, features beneath the outer layers of grime and rotted flesh—New Army soldiers, three of them. They'd been lying in ambush just to snag someone, probably him. But there wasn't a hell of a lot of time to start asking questions as the pistol in the hand of one exploded and a slug tore along Stone's head, gouging out a straight little rivulet of red.

He became unfrozen and flung himself to the side as the other two opened as well, so there was a whole goddamn wall of fire searching for his ass. Stone hit the dirt with the side of his shoulder slamming into something hard, but he kept his momentum and rolled forward and right underneath a still smoldering half-track, its forward tires literally melted into a steaming pile of stinking gunk so that the whole front of the vehicle had sunk down as if on its knees. But Stone didn't have time to worry about the aesthetic ramifications of the hiding place as another row of slugs tore into the dirt just inches from his feet, which he pulled quickly in as he rolled farther under the armored vehicle.

Suddenly there was a howl, and Stone's face grew pale—Excaliber. If the bastards had— He wouldn't even think it. The fucking dog was too smart, too quick for— But the anger instantly cleared his mind, flushing out all the confusion. All right, he had been attacked. Big deal. He had been attacked so many fucking times now, just in the last month or so since he'd emerged from his father's hidden bunker in Colorado's northern mountains, that he couldn't keep track without a calculator. The question was how to attack the attackers.

He rolled twice more on the cold ground as the fusillade continued unabated, slamming into armor. The assholes were obviously willing just to fire away for a while. Well, that was fine with him. Stone quickly scanned the terrain on the other side of the half-track. There wasn't a hell of a lot out there that wasn't burning or just a pile of debris. Stone slid up the side of the vehicle and peeked through a crack in the top armor. There were five of them now—all wearing camouflage uniforms covered with the remains of bodies. And they were closing in, firing constantly as they came forward a few yards apart. They still thought their prey was under the vehicle as their shots slammed into the dirt on the other side or pinged off the armor.

Suddenly he noticed that the 90-mm cannon atop the half-track was aimed straight ahead. Now if the son of a bitch still had a shell left . . . Stone moved quickly forward in a crouch until he reached the small turret. It was hard to tell without getting up there. From here it appeared that the cannon was loaded. The outer firing mechanism was in set position as far as he could see. He could feel that his mind was ready to debate the issue for days, so he pushed himself up with a sudden spring of his legs and clambered up the side of the vehicle. The moment his head appeared, the attackers raised their pistols, trying to find his range. Slugs whistled by each ear. Stone grabbed hold of a bar at the very top of the turret and reached over with the other arm, slamming his palm down on the firing button.

The huge 90-mm exploded out a geyser of smoke as the entire vehicle shook so hard that Stone had to hold on for dear life, dangling from the top of the thing like a monkey from a tree. The huge shell tore out of the ten-foot-long barrel and into the snowy air so hot that it melted a tunnel right through the curtains of white. It traveled the seventy feet or so toward the advancing troops in about one one-hundredth of a second. Then it slammed into the chest of the man in the lead. The high explosives in the shell, meant to take out a tank or the side of a building, instead turned all two hundred and seventeen pounds of elite NAA commando into red spray and a few bones that spun off with the speed of bullets in all directions. The force of the blast expanded out in a circle, catching the remaining four attackers and ripping them into shreds. Arms flew off and faces opened up, revealing everything within them, which poured out as if from a pitcher. Fingers and ears spun off into the air as if madly in search of new bodies that might be in better shape than the ones they had just left.

When Stone finally regained his balance and the armored vehicle stopped shaking enough for him to climb up top and look down, there was nothing left. Nothing human, anyway. Nothing that you would send home to Mother, unless Mother was an undertaker with a fancy for gluing things together again.

CHAPTER
TWO

S TONE HEARD a sound unlike any he had ever encountered in his life. It was somewhere between the wail a hound dog might make if it got a porcupine quill embedded in its nose and the scream an infant emits when it's delivered from the warmth and safety of the womb into a cold, fucked-up world. He instantly knew it was the dog. The bastards who had shot him were gone into hell, but that wasn't going to help Excaliber. With a heavy heart, Stone jumped down the other side of the armored car and rushed toward the sound. It grew louder and shriller with each step until he had to put his hands over his ears, as it was quite painful. And he did start to wonder, as he made his way forward, just how fucked up the pitbull was, in that any animal that could produce a sound so loud and excruciating couldn't be too ready for the grave.

As Stone came to a deep cannon shell—created hole in the ground a good seven feet deep by three wide, he saw that in fact the animal didn't appear hurt at all. Not that he could

9

make out. Except its pride. Evidently it had dived for cover just as Stone had when the first shots were fired—and had chosen what appeared to be a perfect foxhole. Only the hole was over six feet deep and the animal couldn't get out. It stared up at Stone with total and complete mortification on its face, its "kick ass" rep—at least in the pitbull's easily embarrassed psyche—on the line. Stone didn't let himself laugh. He wanted to, but the fixed stare the creature gave him dissuaded him from any such notion. Besides, Stone had no reason to rub it in. He'd been down in that hole too.

"Come on, pal," he said softly to the violently trembling fighting dog, which had calmed down enough to stop its wailings and just let out a few pissed-off grunts. "Grab hold." Stone lowered one end of the NAA utility belt he had grabbed off some dead bastard in the bloody dawn battle. The pitbull snapped its jaw shut hard on the end of the belt and held onto it with all 2400 pounds per square inch that its jaw muscles could exert—the strongest of any canine in the world. Stone braced his legs against a rock a foot away from the edge of the still crumbling hole and pulled up hand over hand. Like a snapping turtle hanging on to a fish meal that's been hooked by someone else, the pitbull emerged from the hole at the end of the belt fishing line, and Stone twisted his body around and deposited his catch on the ground. The dog gave him a twisted little look of thanks and then trotted quickly on, not wanting to discuss the subject any fucking further.

He moved cautiously as he hit the main thoroughfare, now blocked with numerous burning and overturned vehicles, bodies hanging out of them and covering the road, few of them moving. A shell suddenly whistled overhead from far outside the perimeter of the fort, and Stone instinctively dived to the ground, this time grabbing the dog and pulling him down, somewhat unwillingly, to the snow-covered ground. But the shell came down some hundred yards or so past them, falling into a pile of rubble that had already been destroyed once and couldn't get much more atomized. Still, the shell went off with a roar and did its best to grind up the splinters a little more, send a few more particles of the left-overs of war up into the atmosphere.

The attacking forces would probably be leaving now, having laid waste to the place, having taken what still functioning weapons they could haul off. But they wouldn't even be able to use most of them. That was the advantage to having used such a criminal force to attack. For Stone knew that their very anarchistic natures would prohibit them from really being able to put the heavy-duty firepower to any large-scale use, whereas General Patton would have had the ability to conquer the entire country. Unquestionably. The man was a brilliant general, both militarily, in deploying his forces, and in carrying out supply lines. That was why Stone had to stop him. Had to pick the lesser of two evils for the moment. The Fourth Reich could not be allowed to manifest itself.

What was it Patton had said that night they were half drunk together on expensive cognac? "It is my destiny to rule over a perfect order—rid the world of the scum and vermin that make it impossible to progress—and build a society of perfect order. A society modeled on the ants, the bees, those creatures who in their God-given wisdom know that social harmony is more important than the individual." Or some such words. Stone couldn't really remember all that General Patton had said. He had said so much that night. He had taken to Stone, after all, like the son he'd never had. And, with brandy in hand, had told him all of his plans. That was why the betrayal would make him find Stone—and kill him. Unless Stone took out the granite-jawed bastard first.

He made his way along the edges of things, sides of cars, corners of buildings, always on the alert. The pitbull followed at his heels, body spread out and low almost like a cat, neck long, constantly sniffing at the air with pink nostrils constantly scanning every shadow, every mound of burning rubble with all its senses. His breed were fighting pitbulls—bred to take on tigers. Every bit of its sensory apparatus honed by evolution to detect danger, to react even faster than the attacker, faster than a striking tiger. Thus the dog saw the hand suddenly rising from behind an overturned jeep, the metal glistening in its hands from the red and orange rays of a nearby fire roaring high. The pitbull barked sharply to warn Stone and moved its stance forward, like a hunting dog pointing nose-first toward the attacker.

Stone turned in a flash, having been with the animal long enough to know what that particular growl meant. He followed the pointing form and saw the uncertain eyes of an NAA-er, his gun hand wavering for a second between the dog and Stone. His last mistake. As he suddenly realized it was the human he should shoot and started to swing the 9-mm Beretta back around, Stone had already raised his .44 and pulled the trigger. The huge slug ripped into the central portion of the skull at the very instant that the attacker sent the command to his finger to fire. But it never reached the hand. The slug tore into the sniper's head and whipped his brain tissue into an instant mousse, servable at all the best parties. The body crashed backward, the trigger finger as stiff as a piece of rock, the way it would remain forevermore.

"Son of a bitch," Stone muttered under his breath as he let the mag drop back to his side, but he didn't put it away. Everyone was out to get him around here. Mafia crime lords, bikers, toothless bandits, New American Army troops. He might as well just shoot everything he saw, as it was most likely out to do him dirty.

He moved down the street even more cautiously than before. With the smoke and the snow still falling, though more lightly now, and the bodies and burning vehicles everywhere as if World War II had just been dropped into the center of Bradley, it was hard to tell what the hell was going on. Everything seemed to dance and twist in shadows all around him—souls writhing within the twisting columns of smoke. But at last he made it to what was left of Patton's head-quarters—now a heaped pile of timber, blood-soaked rugs, broken furniture. The general had been quite a collector of antiques, paintings, what-all had turned up when his troops went out on search-and-supply missions. All had been brought back to the fort for his personal use. Now it lay smashed, beautiful works of art. It gave Stone's heart a tug to see such beauty destroyed, annihilated. He had seen them and admired them—when Patton and he had been on better terms. There—a Manet, with numerous holes burned through it, lay draped over a cracked support timber. There —a Greek bust with a .45 slug slammed into its mouth so that its sculpted, rock lips were now just dust and the whole center of its face a gouged-out crater like the face of the moon.

Suddenly Stone's heart gave a little skip. For he saw, rolled up like a rug to be taken to the cleaner's, the immense masterpiece the general had given him after his successful mission into the nearby mountains to destroy a horde of bandits. He rushed across the debris, dropped to one knee, and ran his hand across it. No holes, no burn marks. He reached up and unraveled it just a bit to see. Yes—it was the Michelangelo—the Creation—safe and sound. Stone could see the very tip of an angel's finger reaching out through the clouds. It gave him some kind of deep shiver that the paint-ing had survived. It seemed to have been destined to. And Stone felt that as ridiculous as it probably was, it seemed like some kind of honor that he should be entrusted with such a priceless work of art. So much had been destroyed. There wasn't going to be a hell of a lot left for future genera-tions.

He heard a sudden commotion behind him and turned to see the pitbull sighting down on an immense rat that scurried past them with a piece of what looked like human flesh in its sharklike black jaws. The English bullterrier shot forward with all the strength of its pistonlike legs. Excaliber snatched the foot-long rodent up right around the central portion of its body. He snapped down once hard before the creature had time to struggle. The rat's backbone and ribs cracked loudly into splintering pieces like a turkey wing at Thanksgiving dinner. Then the rodent's body was ripped into two parts, and Excaliber opened his mouth and tossed his head hard, flinging the two blood-spewing parts out into the air.

Stone had to jump back to avoid the leaking corpse, but still a piece of it landed on his boot, which totally revolted him, so he bent down, grabbed a broken piece of wallboard, and wiped the slime of rat flesh from his boot. As his eyes came up, his heart nearly fell down to his feet, for a trapdoor had opened in the ground just yards ahead of him, and nine terrified and ash-coated faces were staring straight at him, each man with a pistol in his hand—all aimed straight for Stone's heart.

The dog started to growl, but Stone, without moving a muscle, commanded it sharply to shut up and stay still. Excaliber whimpered and then lay on his paws just behind him, but with his eyes cocked on the men ahead like a lion on a gazelle, ready to move at the slightest threat to his master. Stone scanned the faces back and forth in a single fluid sweep, still keeping his body absolutely still, his gun motionless at his side. It was hard to tell who they were, they were all so filthy, but they looked familiar. Suddenly he realized it was the raw recruits, the men who had just been inducted into the NAA a few days before. Stone had joined the army and gone through the super-intensive New American Army boot camp with them.

"Kill him," one of the men snapped out, starting to raise his pistol. It was Bull. Stone knew the bastard had always hated him since he kicked his ass in a hand-to-hand practice.

"Now listen fellows," Stone started, not having the slightest idea of what he was going to say next.

"You're a traitor," another voice hissed. "Just before General Patton drove off, he said you had brought in the slime. You had betrayed all of us." It was Bo, a trooper Stone had saved from drowning in quicksand. He knew they weren't dying to shoot him or they would have done it already. But he'd have to convince them. All he had to do was convince nine hicks from the sticks who had been inducted into the New American Army that the NAA no longer existed because it had been a fascist force that had to be destroyed. And do it in three seconds.

"Listen, fellows," Stone began again with a weary sigh, wondering just how long he could keep talking his way out of being killed, just how long he could bullshit death itself each time it came to argue with him about why it was time to die.

"No listening, asshole." Bull sneered, raising his .45 toward Stone. "Time to die."

"No," Bo suddenly yelled out, whipping his .45 around toward Bull. "Let him talk," Bo said in a trembling voice. He was obviously terrified of the larger and tougher Bull. "He saved my life. He helped a lot of us in the boot camp. At least he deserves to speak." Bull grumbled and eyed the pistol with a simmering anger, but the others spoke out as well that Stone should have his chance, and the barrel-chested Bull let the big handgun fall away at his side.

"Thanks," Stone said, exhaling a long breath. Excaliber relaxed slightly as Stone did too. The pitbull was linked to his master by an almost telepathic bond. It had been that way from the start. They just knew each other. "Look, I'm not going to lie to you and say I didn't bring down an attack on Fort Bradley, because I did," Stone said. "And I was ready to sacrifice the lives of every man in this camp," Stone said. "I'll admit that too. I was ready to let every one of you smelly bastards kick it. But I had my reasons." They all looked pretty skeptical. But at least they were listening.

"Patton started out with good intentions," Stone went on, "but somewhere along the way he lost it. Because what he has in store for America is the Hitler route. The elimination of blacks, Jews. Hartstein—you're a Jew, right?" Stone asked, looking over at one of the men in the squad. The inductee nodded nervously.

"Hey, pal, fine with me," Stone said. "But someday you might just find yourself up across a wall with the captain of a firing squad asking you if you want a last cigarette. The general wanted to rule by an iron fist. No freedom of the press or religion. Nothing. It wasn't a return to the America we knew but to his own dark vision of hell. You understand what I'm saying?" A few of them seemed to get dim light bulbs glowing in their fear-winced eyes. But most either didn't appear to understand what the hell he was talking about or else didn't particularly give a shit if one race or another got exterminated.

"And," Stone went on, knowing he had to hook them on this. "He had a policy of purification by fire. You know what kind of fire he has in mind?" Stone asked them, glancing around with a smirk as if they were all poor fools. "Atomic fire, my friends. The crazy bastard wants not only to purify America by burning her to a crisp. But right now, today, this minute, he wants to kill me—and he's gone to get a ten-megaton missile to do it. You hear what I'm saying. You can kill me or not—it hardly matters. Because he won't know it. And unless we stop him first, you're all dead men."

That seemed to get their attention. Even Bull looked a little pale through his ash makeup.

"Let me get this straight," the big man said skeptically as the others gulped continuously, their Adam's apples moving up and down like corks on rough water. "You telling me that at any motherfuckin' second some big ol' missile gonna come down right on our heads?"

"That's about the size of it," Stone said with a razor-sharp smile. The trapdoor flew back and the entire crew—all ten of them, he could see now—stepped out and up onto the rubble. Just a few seconds before they had been ready to kill him—and now . . . But time passes and things change. And no man likes the idea of his radioactive balls spinning endlessly through space.

CHAPTER

THREE

"SIR," ONE of the ash-coated recent inductees said, looking at Stone. "Should we call you sir?"

"No," Stone said, waving his hand with a disgusted look. "Just Stone . . . will do fine." He looked them over quickly. They looked like shit. They hadn't particularly known what to do just days before when he had gone through the two-day boot camp with them. And he was sure that they hadn't learned a hell of a lot since then, either. They were scared too. Hell, most of them were just kids, not even out of their teens. Half of them weren't even holding their pistols correctly. It wasn't a hell of a lot to work with. But then, beggars . . .

"At ease," Stone said with a sheepish look as he saw them trying to stand at some semblance of attention. There was something in him that just didn't take well to telling men what to do. His childhood, most likely. His father being military had a lot to do with that. And the fact that he and his dad had fought their entire lives until the day the Major died. And yet many of his father's words remained in Stone's mind to this day—words of a man who had seen much. "If you want men to follow, you have to enthuse them," Stone remembered the Major telling a fellow officer once over a prime rib roast at their home in Denver. "Have to make them believe that they're special, hot shit, God's gift to the United States fighting forces." Stone took a deep breath and prepared to lie his ass off.

"Tell me, fellows, how come you were down in that junk hole, anyway?" Stone asked them as they stood side by side in a vague sort of line. They had just been learning military ways for under a few weeks now and had only just begun to get the hang of it—barely. Well, Stone wasn't one for marching or spit-and-polish, thank God.

"'Cause this major man tol' us to guard it," one of them said. Stone tried to remember his name. Or any of them, for that matter. "Said to stay down here and guard the general's stuff, and if any asshole shows up—to fill his ass full of lead. And those were his exact words," the half-wit said with a smile, proud that he could remember so much vital information. It was all Stone could do not to just walk away. But he had to have men. There was no way in hell he would be able to attack Patton with the kind of defensive forces the general had at his command, without some kind of fighting team.

"Well, you did real good," Stone said, looking around the place. "Look's like no one got in here—other than the artillery shells—but then you couldn't do much about that, anyway, could you?" He laughed nervously, knowing it sounded crazy as the recruits glanced at each other. "Yes, fine job."

"But no one really tried to get in here—uh—sir," one of the real young ones, tall and lanky, his face still acned, said nasally.

"Ah, but they didn't try, because somehow they sensed you all. And knew that they were dead men if they stepped one foot in here. Every man has a sixth sense about danger

—even if it's only partially developed. They *knew*—that's all—just knew that there were some tough-ass troops lying in wait." The men, fortunately for Stone, were young or dumb enough, or both, to be extremely gullible, and so they smiled at the praise of their manhood. "And that's why you guys are kick-ass soldiers. I knew it from the start—back in training. Could see that I was working with a fine bunch of men." Somewhere inside themselves they probably all knew he was lying, but every man likes to be complimented, to be told he is tough. Thus they smiled even wider, stood a little straighter, and decided that this guy Stone wasn't such a bad son of a bitch, after all. And Stone learned the basic truth that all politicians know instinctively—that lying works.

"Now, let me just say two things about my running this show," Stone said, trying to sound firm. "One—we're not going to worry about parades, clothes, haircuts, fingernails, or saying 'sir' or any of that shit, okay? You guys can pick your noses and eat it for all I care. But two—you've got to do what I tell you, when I tell you. Not just because I want you to but because the lives of every man on this attack force will be dependent on every other man. You're all in this together. You understand? Any one of us goes and ka-boom—it could be all over. And if we don't get Patton—it's going to be kaboom, anyway, for this whole damned central part of the country. So we have to move fast and hard. I'm not going to mislead you—it's going to be a bloodbath. You hear me? We're going into hell. So if any of you want to back out now, just tell me—because I have to know I can count on whoever's on the trip when the shit hits the fan."

"Sir." Another of them spoke up, though who it was Stone couldn't begin to tell, as the man looked like the inside of a vacuum cleaner, covered with dust and soot. "I guess the fact is, most of us grew up in these parts. And, well, I don't know who's right or wrong in all this, I guess, but I don't want to see my daddy's farm tore up to hell into that there rad-active, whatever you calls it, stuff." The others nodded in agreement, even Bull, who Stone knew was the one he was going to have to keep his eye on. The guy kept giving him funny looks.

"Good," Stone said enthusiastically. "Then we're in this until the fat lady sings. All right, then—we gotta get things going. First, I can't even remember all of your names. So tell me who you are, and what—if any—special training of weapons you know about." Stone looked at the man on the far right side of the ragged line who looked around, down, at the men next to him, back at Stone, back down at the ground, up at Stone, and then asked, "Me?"

"Yeah, pal," Stone said with a grimace. "You."

"Oh, well, I'm Nathan Farber, come from Greenwood, other side of the state. Far as any trainin'—well, I's good as a mother with a knife. Can skin a deer—or a man's throat."

"I'll keep that in mind," Stone said. "Next."

"Ross Phillips," the man said, "from Brandon. Don't know a hell of a lot about weapons," the man said, "but good with a truck, drove one for this guy. Can shift gears, everything."

"Gary—Gary Zzychinski," the next said, "from Greeley. Done a lot of hunting. Used .22 and 30-30. These here M16s suck, but get me something good and I'll knock a squirrel out of a fucking tree—or just take his balls off if you want." Stone grinned and moved his attention to the next man.

"Trevor Simpson, sir," the guy barked out, keeping his back straight, looking more like a soldier than the others. "From Rangely, sir. Knowledge of explosives. Used to help set them for a mining operation—before things got bad. Know nitro, fuses, timers, you name it. Show it to me—I'll blow it up for you." The man seemed a little older than the others—more intelligent.

"Excellent," Stone said, slapping the man on the shoulder and making a mental note to keep this guy on tap. His services were undoubtedly going to be needed soon. So it went along the line, coming finally to the last guy there, Bull. Stone could feel himself tense up as their eyes met. He knew the bastard hated his fucking guts.

"You know me," the man said. He was a good four inches taller than Stone and probably fifty to sixty pounds heavier. But though he scared the others, Stone had already knocked him down. The guy hadn't forgotten.

"Hope there's no hard feelings," Stone said, holding out his hand.

"Nah," the man said, taking the offered hand. "Bygones are bygones—got to take care of business. I ain't no idiot, much as I might sound like one." For some reason Stone's hackles went up at the words. They sounded out of character for the man, revealing more self-analysis or awareness of his outward appearance than Stone would have thought him to have.

"And believe it or not, I know something about communications equipment. They had already started training me to be a corps signalman, carrying radio pack and all. So if we can dig up any, then you got yourself a comm man."

"Good, Bull," Stone said. "I'm glad to see that you're man enough to be beyond all that bullshit." He knew the son of a bitch was lying. And he knew Bull knew he knew. . . . But they smiled at each other like account execs at a cocktail party. Typical communications between members of the human species.

"All right, then," Stone said, slapping his hands together as if they were really getting somewhere. Then he remembered that his father had often done that and instantly stopped, sort of holding the hands out in midair, not quite knowing what to do with them. "The first thing we'll do is just what Bull said—dig up something. Let's spread out and scout up what gear we can. Look for big stuff, mobile artillery, armored vehicles. Even if it looks fucked up, make note. Then we can check it all out. Try to find automatic weapons. I know there were some Steyr 5.56-mm assault rifles, that the general had just received—crates of them. We're going to need heavy-duty firepower, so forget anything small. Grenades, grenade launchers, hand-held rockets would all be useful. Break up into groups of two—we'll meet back here in half an hour. And keep your fucking eyes open, 'cause there's assholes shooting at anything that moves out there."

They broke up and headed off, Stone taking the dog and one of the other men, Bo, who he had been friendly with in boot camp and who, though not terribly smart, seemed trustworthy. And Stone was going to need someone he could trust. Because he didn't even know for sure if these sons of bitches were going to come back with weapons to help him —or to kill him.

CHAPTER

FOUR

TWO HOURS later Stone stood in the center of a pile of equipment that the men had dragged, pulled, or wheeled back. He had the raw recruits arm themselves with the 5.56-mm assault rifles, which were in perfect condition and fresh out of the crates—with enough ammo to give each man twenty thirty-round magazines. There was also a box of grenades, a flamethrower, and various assorted other items that he had them load up with. Most of the vehicles he was unhappy to find had either already been knocked out in the barrage of the fort or stolen by the enemy forces and taken back to their squalid little hideouts in the mountains where the half-tracks, the jeeps, the tanks would more than likely be the centerpieces of the whole rotten show and would just stand there and rust for the next fifty years.

But it was the scouting report that interested him most. One of the teams had gone to the northern perimeter of the smoking fortress to search for supplies and had heard some heavy machinery rumbling around. They had gone outside and seen three tanks manned by Guardians of Hell just sort of wheeling around back and forth on a large, open field. "Like they was playing bumper cars or something," the man, Bannister, reported.

Stone looked them all over, now that they were cleaned up a little and armed. They still looked like shit—and their first blood battle was about to come up. He had hoped to have a little time to work with them on the way north as they tried to track down Patton. But as usual fate wasn't about to hand out any Get Out of Jail Free cards. He glanced over at the two jeeps and one transport truck that the men had scrounged up. At first he had been glad to have them—any vehicle was welcome—but now that there was the chance to get working tanks... For Stone knew the power of the supermodern Bradley IIIs, with their 120-mm cannon and mini-missile systems, their laser sights. If they could get their hands on a few of them, it might make all the difference. Especially since the general was bound to have a whole shitload of the war wagons stashed somewhere else. Shit, the whole thing seemed impossible every time he thought about it. So he didn't think about it.

"We gotta get those tanks," he said as they kneeled in a circle every man loaded to the hilt with firepower. "And I think I know how." Slowly and carefully, enunciating every word so they understood just what he had in mind, Stone told them his plan, and though they stared back a little wild-eyed at him, no one objected. Or had the guts to say that they did.

An hour later Stone crawled through some bushes at the top of a rise and took out his binoculars. There certainly wasn't any problem finding them—the bikers were making enough noise to wake the dead in the next county. There were about thirty of the Guardians of Hell in their usual black leather jackets loaded down with chains. They lay on the slope about two hundred feet below Stone as they chugged bottles of liquor and laughed uproariously at the goings-on in front of them. Stone had never seen tanks playing chicken before, but these guys, Stone had to admit, as slimy and murderous as they were, knew how to have fun.

On a long, cleared field, two of the Bradley IIIs were revving up at opposite ends. The third tank by the side was loaded down with Guardians draped all over the thing in various states of drunken bliss. The parked tank shot its cannon, the barrel aimed at the center of the fortress, and the entire Bradley shook violently as the shell exploded out. It was apparently the starting signal for the fun and games, for the two tanks shifted into gear and, with a loud roar of engines not being worked quite right, came tearing toward each other. There was about a hundred yards separating the two, which gave them enough time to accelerate as they drove forward. Stone watched, fascinated, at the same time with a sick feeling in his stomach, since if they damaged the battle machines, his whole plan was going to be nipped in the bud.

The two thundering vehicles sending up a cloud of dust behind them came charging toward each other like two rogue elephants ready to do battle over territorial rights. They both seemed to be trying to go faster, but it was clear by the constant grinding sounds coming from the tanks that they didn't quite know how to operate them. The tanks came right up on each other, neither one veering off. If this was chicken, neither of the bikers inside wanted to be the one to cluck. The Bradleys smashed into each other with a crunching sound, and both were instantly enveloped in a cloud of dust. When it had cleared, Stone could see that the one coming from his right had caught the other just at the front corner and spun it around nearly 180 degrees. Both cannons still seemed to be functioning. But it couldn't go on—a few more crashes and the things would be valueless. It was now or never.

Stone wriggled backward a few yards and flipped over onto his back. He waved his hand up and down, and a hundred yards or so down the other side of the slope, Ross, the youngest, and hopefully the fastest, of his attack force, saw the "go" sign and sprinted off as fast as his legs could carry him. Stone got to his feet and tore ass down the hill and over to where the action was about to take place. But first the trap had to be set and the prey lured into it.

Ross, stripped down to T-shirt, cotton khakis, and sneakers, ran up to what had once been one of the side entrances to the fort, now a collapsed row of fencing and barricades. He jumped up on top of a bomb-created mound a good eight feet high with a bloody foot sticking out of the bottom of it and, making sure he was in clear sight of the tanks and the bikers, cupped his hands over his mouth.

"Hey, assholes," Ross yelled out, enjoying this even though his heart was threatening to pound right through his chest. "Hey, assholes, hey, assholes . . ." He had to yell it five times before they really heard him. Then there was an instantaneous silence as every biker fell quiet, their bottles dangling in their hands; even the three tanks shut their engines off so they could hear what all the commotion was about.

"What was that you said, twerp?" the nearest Guardian of Hell, only about fifty yards away from the teenage soldier, yelled back, wiping his hand across his mouth in disbelief.

"You heard me," Ross screamed back again, so scared now that he suddenly got afraid he might lose control of his bladder. He had never had fifty ugly, scarred faces staring at him with nothing but death in their eyes. But there was no turning back now—that was for damned sure. "I said, hey, assholes. That is the proper way to address you, isn't it?" Ross felt satisfied with that statement. It had a certain ring to it.

"Kid, I killed so many of your fucking guys today"—the biker laughed out with a hoarse cough as he gulped down a huge draft of the rotgut whiskey he was drinking—"that I'm going to pretend I didn't hear that and let you live. That is, if you turn around right now and run as fast as your fucking legs can carry you."

"Now why would I want to run from a syphilitic pansy like you and all your other ugly pig friends?" the teen yelled back. If Ross had been searching for the right words to get things going—create a little emotional fire, as it were—he succeeded beyond his wildest expectations, as to a man the bikers leapt to their feet and ripped out pistols and rifles of every size and caliber. Ross didn't wait to see the next act but turned and ran, as their hands were still fumbling wildly for their weapons. He tore ass straight back into the fortress, leaping madly over burning debris, stiffening corpses in their own little private pools of blood. A fusillade of slugs slammed into the mound where he had been standing, sending little puffs of dirt into the air. The entire bunch of bikers started toward the little worm who had dared insult them, but stopped after a few yards of huffing and puffing as the tanks roared back into life and all three of them lurched forward, treads spinning like they were trying to get airborne. The bikers were big, most of them going two-fifty, three hundred, and more. So they came to stumbling stops as the Bradleys tore past them, out for blood.

Ross ran for his life past what had been the open training field. The battle machines were moving a little faster than he had thought and were already at the side gate, while he was only halfway across. One of the huge 120-mm cannons suddenly roared, and he flinched involuntarily, wincing and waiting for the explosive sledgehammer to descend on his head. But though the Guardians driving the tank had figured how to fire the thing, they still hadn't quite mastered the aiming of it. The shell took off straight over the ruins of Patton's fortress and didn't come down for five miles, where it took out about ten square feet of desert in a funnel of dust and smashed rock. The shot, if anything, slammed a whole quart of adrenaline into Ross's legs, and he surged ahead like a sprinter in the hundred-yard dash at the Olympics.

The tanks came right over the fence, crushing it beneath their treads, grinding it up and sending it out behind them like something ready for the scrap heap. They rode over the debris and the bodies, following in Ross's footsteps as they headed deeper into the remains of Fort Bradley.

Ross reached the first of the barracks that were still standing and relaxed for the first time in the last five minutes. He tore between the two buildings, one of them partially collapsed, the other burned out inside but with walls and roof still intact. He slowed slightly to make sure they didn't lose him, but as he saw the cloud of dust coming right down the main thoroughfare, he tore ass again. The three tanks came up to the barracks and surged forward, searching for the little bastard who was about to die. The long cannon of each Bradley swiveled up and down and from side to side as those inside tried frantically to sight up the little cocksucker who was now only about fifty yards ahead.

Suddenly, from the rooftops of the buildings on each side of them, men jumped down and onto the speeding tanks. Two on the first; three on the second; three, including Stone, on the third. They grabbed for dear life onto whatever handholds they could find as the big war wagons lurched and shook like Brahma bulls beneath them. Stone grabbed hold of the hatchway and pulled hard. Thank God the bastards wouldn't even think of sealing themselves off—the one thing he had been praying for. Why should they? Who the hell was about to attack a tank?

Stone lifted the armored steel cover as Bo, hanging on just feet away at the other side of the opening, heaved a grenade inside. Ahead, the attack team did the same in each of the tanks. Stone ducked down and covered his head with the side of his arm as a loud pop came from inside and a rush of acrid smoke exploded from the top as if from a chimney. The smell made Stone gag for a second, and he turned his head to avoid a full whiff of the nausea gas. He pulled out his Luger .44 and held it in his right hand, the left clenched tightly around a handle built into the top of the battle machine. The tank suddenly seemed to slow dramatically and then spun to the right, where it crashed into the side of a small shed, leveled the structure, and came to a shuddering halt. Stone saw one of his team fall beneath the treads of the tank just ahead of them, but his eyes shot back to the hatchway next to him from which a greasy-haired head was emerging.

The Guardian came out firing, his finger squeezing down on a sawed-off 12-gauge pump. He got one blast off, which shot straight up toward the clouds before Stone's Redhawk spoke. The slug tore into the biker's throat like a guillotine, slicing through the larynx, the jugular. A sheet of red sprayed out over the top of the dark green metal, and the biker seemed to rise up from the opening, as if being launched from it, and rolled down over the side onto the ground. Another head emerged, this one trying to get his .38 into firing position. But as the pistol rose up, sighting for Stone's chest, Bo, still dangling from the opposite side of the tank, slammed the muzzle of his army-issue .45 right up against the slime's skull and pulled. For Stone, who was staring directly into the biker's boil-pocked face, it appeared to disintegrate suddenly—the nose, the lips, all melting like a plastic doll on fire. Then the face actually shot toward him, as if being sent special delivery, and Stone had to duck to avoid the bloody cargo.

The body somehow climbed another step or two on twitching legs and seemed almost to dive over the edge of the Bradley, as if trying out for the school swimming team. Stone waited for a second to see if anyone else was surfacing, and seeing nothing, he started down into the machine. He was but halfway down the ladder when he heard a click and looked down to see a Guardian pointing a pistol straight up at him. Stone squeezed himself against the rungs as the biker fired and the slug tore so close to Stone's back that he could feel the heat of it go by. There wasn't room or time for him to fire, so he slipped both hands around the steel ladder and slid right down the thing.

His heavy boot slammed into the biker's skull just as the oversize killer was getting ready for squeeze number two on his Luger. But the boot, coming down with the very edge of the steel-plated heel into the top of the slime's head, dug into the skull, cracking right through it so that a bloody line appeared across the whole top of the scalp. Stone lifted the leg and brought it down again. This time the skull completely split open, the hair-covered bone cracking apart like a badly broken egg. Brain tissue and blood and God knew what else was stored up in a man's head all exploded out, covering Stone's boots and the innards of the tank with a piece of his mind.

The biker dropped to the floor of the war machine where he lay jerking, his pistol still in his right hand, the finger still trembling as it pulsed with the last command the brain had ever sent out—to fire. Stone, knowing the man was no longer a threat, scanned the inside of the tank, but that was it. This one, at least, was deloused, and still functioning. He kicked the quivering corpse out of the way and slid into the driver's seat. All the systems were still on, and as far as Stone could see, everything was working. The entire system was computer-controlled, and constant readouts of the readiness of the Bradley's component systems were being scrolled on a computer screen just over the front control panel.

Stone slammed the controls for the video camera to do a 360 and quickly saw that his men seemed to have the situation at least relatively under control. Dead bodies lay around the other tanks, both of which had stopped in their tracks, and it was *his* men who were standing atop them, victorious. The first battle had gone well—better than he could have hoped. But as the camera reached the end of its sweep— back to the field and the side gate—Stone saw a whole slew of the bikers, who hadn't been able to keep up with the

Bradley's, walking slowly toward them. Unaware that anything untoward had happened, they wanted to witness the rest of the fun. Wanted to see the little twerp with the death wish who had insulted them. Wanted to see him die.

Stone reached for the cannon controls and swiveled the turret all the way around. Through the periscope-type, laser-sighted viewfinder that lowered automatically in front of his eyes, he sighted up the approaching crowd of leather-jacketed scum of the earth. He waited until the three red lines crisscrossed over one another—he had the face of the lead biker dead in his sights. Then he fired. The cannon pulled back on his treads, as if about to take a great jump forward, and the barrel spat out a shell the size of a man's leg. There was a tremendous roar, even louder against the relative silence of what had just been a killing ground, and the projectile whistled into the bikers like a bowling ball of death looking for some human pins to take down.

Stone couldn't even really see just what happened. There was a cloud of dirt and blood and arms and unrecognizable things, and that was that. About ten bodies lay in various states of disintegration for a circle of thirty feet around the blast crater. The rest of the bikers ran backward, slowly, confused at first. And then, as they saw the cannon start swiveling again, tracking them, they tore ass. For a bunch of three-hundred-pounders they moved surprisingly fast as they disappeared out of the fortress walls and back into the woods with the other animals.

CHAPTER

FIVE

R ANDOLPH WAS dead. Stone hadn't exchanged two words with the guy. And now, lying as he was, his chest all opened up from a shotgun blast from a biker before he, in turn, was blasted to bits, Randolph didn't look like he had much to say. The rest of the men seemed both proud that they had actually been able to carry out Stone's plan and a little pale around the gills that one of their own had bought it so quickly. But if any of them was having second thoughts, they kept it to themselves.

"You did good," Stone said, addressing them as they stood in a ragged line in front of him. "Real good. You should all be proud of yourselves. Those bastards"—he glanced at the corpses of the bikers, which lay all over the place like bloody mannequins that had been tossed from a department store that was going out of business—"were tough. Real tough. I've faced them before. So whatever doubts you had about your own abilities to carry out this mission—well, you just proved 'em wrong."

Stone turned around and faced the grave that had been so hastily dug. The torn body of the dead recruit lay wrapped in an American flag that someone had grabbed down from a pole. Stone knew that rituals mattered when it came to fighting—and dying. At least the men under him would know that if they went out, they'd die like men, would be buried under the dirt rather than just lying out there to be consumed by beasts and maggots. It wasn't much—and yet he knew that for them it mattered. Anthropologists defined the transition from barbarism to civilization by, among other things, the moment when man had started burying his dead. Started wrapping them in shawls, putting strange relics on their faces and bodies—an evolution that showed that man was different from the animals. That he had a soul.

"Dear Lord, or whoever's up there," Stone said, his head bowed as the other men stood behind him, looking solemn. "Take this poor son of a bitch up there into your clouds. I don't know what this man did in the past, probably some good and some bad things. But I know that today he gave his life fighting for the light, fighting against the darkness that threatens to take our whole land down into hell. Whatever else was inside of him—in his final moments—there was bravery and a willingness to make the final sacrifice on the side of life." Stone coughed, not quite knowing how to end the makeshift paean to the beyond. "Uh, thanks," he said, and then lifted his head to signal that the ceremony was over.

The body was lowered into the ground, and dirt quickly shoveled over it. In seconds it had returned to that from which it had sprung. Stone looked around at the other men, who seemed moved by his words. At least they weren't laughing.

"All right, we got work to do," he said brusquely, suddenly embarrassed by his chaplain duties. "Hartstein, Simpson, and you, Bull," he said, looking around the group, which stared back with curious eyes, wondering just what the hell the man they had entrusted with their lives had in store for them next. But there was respect in their eyes now, where before there had just been fear and hostility. He had led them into the face of death, and they were still farting and burping. So far, so good. Stone led the three of them off to one of the three tanks that stood in the center of the ruins of Fort Bradley as the other men got their gear back on and sat around throwing sticks, which Excaliber, glad for a little sport, fetched and brought back.

Inside the Bradley III, Stone sat at the controls of the battle wagon and put on the headset.

"All right, I picked you three, because frankly you're the smartest of the lot as far as I can see. Now, what I'm going to do is teach you to run this motherfucker—in one easy lesson. All right?" He didn't wait for an answer and didn't see the expressions of sheer incredulity as the three of them looked quickly around at the array of flashing lights and readout panels, at the seemingly countless buttons and dials that filled the control panel in front of Stone.

"Now, it's just like driving a car, right? You've all driven cars before, I pray," Stone asked rhetorically, not even waiting for the answers. "You just flip this little switch here, then turn this systems-on lever here, then you . . ." Slowly he went through all the guidance mechanisms of the Bradley, praying that he even remembered it all correctly himself. He had only driven the tank two times, and then only for a few hours each time. But everything basically seemed to work, and the damned thing at least didn't blow up in their faces. When he had finished and turned around and saw the looks of utter consternation on their faces, Stone went through it all again. After the second time they at least looked like they knew how to press a button, and he threw the tank into gear and took off down the center of the still smoking fort.

Stone put the war wagon through its paces. He wanted them not to just know how to operate the thing but also to understand its myriad capabilities. He went slow, he went fast, taking the tank up to its top speed of forty-plus miles per hour. He brought the Bradley to a screeching stop and then turned on a dime, showing them how to operate the treads on one side only, giving the Bradley enormous maneuverability.

Then he let them try it. To say the least, each was hesitant to actually drive the thing, and they kept looking around at Stone with apprehensive expressions. But after they had had their shot for about half an hour each, Stone took the controls and brought the Bradley back to where the rest of the attack force was waiting.

"Well," he said when they all had climbed out and were staring up at the huge death machine, somewhat amazed that they had just been operating it, "what do you think? Can you drive the fucking thing?" None of them said no, though he could see in their inability to look him right in the eyes that they had their doubts. But all he wanted was for them to be able to get the things going. They could learn the finer points on the road. Next Stone had three more of the men accompany him, telling them also that they were the three cleverest fellows of the lot and that he had chosen them to be the gunners. In fact, one of the main features of the Bradley III was its central control operation. The driver of the tank could also fire every one of its weapons systems. But it would take weeks for them to have even minimal abilities at running the whole show. Besides, with one man driving and one on cannon, there was less opportunity for betrayal. For Stone, though he was trying to act like they were all just one big happy fighting unit, still didn't trust them. And he could hardly blame them for not trusting him.

Half an hour later three tanks lumbered out of the fort, three men to a tank. Stone had Bo and Simpson with him, the two men he trusted the most. At least he wouldn't have to keep wondering if one of them was about to pull a gun behind him and blast his brains out. He figured if worse came to worst and he saw one of the turrets swinging toward him, he'd be faster. It was great working with guys you liked. Stone was in constant communication with the other drivers, talking to them, reassuring them, giving them instructions over the built-in headset. The tanks followed the main road and then just went up and over the piles of debris at the edge of the fort. Stone had had some of the men help him hoist the Harley up onto the back of one of the Bradleys, raising and locking it back with a built-in pulley system.

Excaliber was at first skittish about being in the tank. He didn't seem to take kindly to the lights flashing, the smell of plastic from the panel. And for the first half hour or so he emitted a constant low growl, which got on everyone's nerves. But at last he found a nice warm spot at the back above the engine and curled up in a corner and went right to sleep, with a final jaw-cracking yawn and a little bark for Stone, to say: Wake me when the shooting starts.

Stone went slowly at first, hardly getting above fifteen miles per hour. He knew he was pushing it to the limit by even hoping Hartstein and Bull could handle the things. Stone kept the viewing system in full 360-degree perspective. The screen above him split automatically into four parts, giving him vision of all four quadrants of the terrain around him and the two tanks following behind. The heavily armed battle machines seemed to dance all over the place behind him, turning, slowing down, speeding up, skidding sideways from time to time. But somehow they kept going.

The first sign of trouble was when Stone suddenly heard a yell over the earphone on his head, a sound of such volume that his face turned white. He slammed his hand down on the cannon controls, ready to aim the big gun and take out whoever was about to spring some trick. But as his eyes focused on the monitor above him, Stone saw with horror that one of the tanks had run right off an embankment and was lodged against some boulders at almost a ninety-degree angle.

"Halt, halt," he yelled over the radio, and the tank that was following came to an abrupt, gear-grinding stop. Stone wheeled his Bradley around and shot over to where the battle wagon had tumbled. He pulled to a stop, threw the whole thing into neutral, and dashed up the ladder for a close-up view. It was both better and worse than he had feared. The crew was still alive and the tank still seemed structurally whole, but the damned thing was balanced on a few rocks that didn't look all that big. And below them was a hundred-foot drop onto solid granite. He could hear the men inside yelling bloody murder and could see by the way the Bradley III was shifting around that they were desperately trying to climb out.

"Don't move!" Stone screamed out at the top of his lungs. "You hear me, you bastards in there? Don't move a fucking inch! You're on the edge of a cliff—you hear me? Every step is bringing you closer to going over—to being dead men." If his words didn't do it, a sudden shift in the position of the tank did. One of the rocks holding the thing up had fallen free, and the whole tank shuddered and moved six inches farther down. The movement inside the tank stopped, and Stone leaned down over the very edge and yelled down to the men.

"Look, I promise I'll get you out of there—just stay loose. Play cards, jerk off, but don't try to get out of there —you understand?"

"Understand," a voice yelled back. "Just get us the fuck off this cliff." Stone jumped up and tore back to his tank, shooting down the ladder and back to the controls. He brought the tank up until it was just a yard or so from the precipice and gave orders for the other to follow suit—very, very slowly. But Bull, who was driving, seemed to have a knack for the vehicle and pulled up right alongside Stone, just a few yards away. Thick cables were quickly pulled out of storage and attached to the front steel posts of the two tanks. Stone, not wanting to be responsible for any more deaths, took the other ends of the two steel cables over the side himself, with a rope around his waist and held by three of the men. It took about twenty minutes, but at last he surveyed the arrangement, decided he couldn't do anything more, and got back in the tank.

"Okay, real slow, you got me?" Stone said to Bull over the radio. "We got to move together or we're going to tilt the thing off-balance. Set her for minimum speed, use the gearshift on your left—you see it, marked 'Low Drive 5'?"

"Copy," Bull said back. Stone was getting to like the bastard he trusted least. At least the guy seemed to know what the hell he was doing.

"Let's do it," he said. Slowly, moving an inch at a time, the treads of the two tanks edged slowly backward. There was a loud groaning sound as the cables stretched so taut, Stone was afraid they would pop. But although it almost seemed that the fallen Bradley III didn't really want to come back up, hardly budging at first, as the cable reached its tension limit, the tank started crawling backward up the almost sheer face of the drop. Stone could feel the engine of his war wagon screaming out in protest, but it kept pumping out the power. And at last, after five heart-stopping minutes, the fallen tank reached its balance point on the edge of the ravine and suddenly slammed down onto the dirt with a thunderous crash.

The men inside came flying out the hatch, as if it were on fire inside, and jumped out onto the earth. One of the men, Farber got down on his hands and knees and kissed sweet terra firma. They came over and slapped Stone and Bull on the backs over and over, their faces wide with the smiles that those who had just escaped imminent death wear. And though it took nearly half an hour to convince them to get back inside, at last the whole show was on the road again. Hartstein promised to drive more carefully. And Stone, only half in jest, told him he was going to take the son of a bitch's driver's license away "if there are any more moving violations."

CHAPTER

SIX

SOON THE three-tank convoy was moving again, Stone driving very slowly in the lead, hardly rising above fifteen miles per hour for the first hour or so. He had been pushing them all too fast. Both Hartstein and Bull kept asking Stone questions over the headset. "What does this do?" "What does that do?" Stone had decided not to show them how to work the missile system. Each Bradley III had six ground-to-ground, or ground-to-air, heat-seeking missiles—with ninety-five percent kill performance. But Stone, following the Major's advice—"Always have a trick up your sleeve"—wanted to keep the operation of the mini-max missile system to himself.

The tanks left the semi-mountainous area where Fort Bradley had been built and headed out onto a more prairie-like terrain. Here, at lower altitude, the snow had left only a fine coating, and the tanks spat up huge funnels of dust that joined above them, forming a cloud that followed behind for miles. Cacti grew everywhere, rising up like spiked fingers pointing to the sky, to God, or whatever lay hidden up there. Fields of them, green and black, towering above the tanks on all sides. They came to an incline from which Stone could see for miles in each direction over the flat terrain, and he called for the attack convoy to come to a stop.

"It's target-practice time, gentlemen," Stone said. "Now, Zzychinski and Phillips, you're both the gunnery men. Switch on the speak switch on your headsets so you can ask me questions. I've shown you basically how to operate the 120-mm cannon system and the 50-cal twin machine guns. But now I want to give you a little hands-on practice. We'll do static firing first, then mobile. Hartstein, come up alongside me on the far side, Bull on the near, and face the direction my tank is pointing." They followed his command, and after about thirty seconds the three tanks stood side by side, their cannons all facing forward over miles of cacti and anthills.

"Now, whatever you do, do it slow and careful. 'Cause we're working with live ammo—heavy-duty ammo, at that. The shells that these Bradleys fire are superconcentrated high explosive—probably the most punch per square inch of anything short of field nukes. Now, using your laser range-finding system, look into the sighting mechanisms until you have those three tall cacti standing almost right next to each other. About a mile off. See them?"

"Yeah," they both replied.

"Okay. Sight up. When you have the three red lines pinpointing it, fire." Suddenly the tank to the left roared and emitted a screaming projectile. The shell came down just short of the cactus trio and sent up a little tornado of dirt. Then Bull's tank rocked back on its treads, and the 120-mm burped out a mouthful of death. The shell slammed right into the top of the cactus, but for some reason it didn't detonate. Instead it sliced right through one of them like a scythe, about five feet from the top, and then flew on past, exploding a good two miles off. The severed head of cactus slowly leaned over and then tumbled down where it crashed into pulpy pieces on the ground.

They both fired again, having shifted the long cannon barrels. This time both shells slammed dead center of the growth near the base. All three cacti just seemed to disintegrate in the air as if bursting from the insides out, as pieces of them spun off in every direction. When the noise and dust settled, there wasn't a thing above the base, above a few feet off the ground.

"Not bad," Stone said over the radio, swiveling the video around in search of some other targets. "There," he said suddenly. "Swing turrets around to the left, say about twenty degrees. See that anthill? Son of a bitch must be twenty-five feet tall, over there about a mile and a half." They both muttered assent, and again Stone had them open up. This time Zzychinski found target acquisition the first time, with Phillips's shell coming in right behind his, creating a second explosion within the already boiling air of sand and scorched ants and forming a halo of particles a good hundred feet around. Stone had them take out a few more structures of nature. He didn't feel overjoyed about just randomly taking out all this stuff. But there was more where that came from. If a ten-meg, or a few of them, went off in Colorado, there wouldn't be shit. He had to teach these guys to actually be able to use the tanks. They would be facing elite troops, elite armored units. In tank battle the first shot was often the last.

"All right, you're not too bad with stationary targets," Stone said after they'd blasted various structures into nonexistence. "Unfortunately none of the bastards we're going to be fighting will be stationary. So now we'll try some mobile firing. Drivers, in combat situations the gunner takes command. You listen to him." They started forward, Stone in the lead, going through desolate flatlands with the fields of cacti and anthills off to their left. "Black cactus with three arms at a half mile," Stone yelled into the mouthpiece. Within seconds both gunners had found the target, and their cannons erupted almost simultaneously. One of the shells crashed down about ten yards past, the second just a yard or so in front.

"Again," Stone screamed. "You missed—that's a tank—he's going to blow your ass up. Take that motherfucker out. Fire, and don't stop until—" But he hadn't even finished his harangue when both barrels screamed out tongues of flames, once, twice, three times—a total of six high-explosive shells. Stone kept them moving ahead at about twenty miles per hour while he sighted up to observe the damage. They had not only taken out the offending vegetation but had gouged out a swimming pool–size hole where the vanished cactus had just stood.

They were doing a hell of a lot better than he had expected. And they were competing with each other—each tank's crew striving to do better than the other. Still, they'd have to do a lot better than that. He had no illusions about the enemy they were facing, three Bradleys against perhaps fifty, against a heavily armored fortress—this time on the alert. It was insane, it was impossible. Stone knew the odds against him were something no betting man would take. But if he had worried about the odds, Stone would have just laid in a corner and gone to sleep.

CHAPTER

SEVEN

NIGHT FELL suddenly like a veil dropping over the earth. In the twilight even Stone found it difficult going. As the stars started snapping on across the skies, Stone pulled his troops to a stop just as they approached more foothills. They had been getting all the breaks so far, and Stone didn't want to push it. He bivouacked them into a half-circle with their backs to a sheer rock wall and set a guard. Then the men cooked, and after dinner a crate of hidden beer was pulled out. They looked at Stone, wondering if he was going to nix the after-dinner imbibing. But he spat and looked away. Like he had told them he wasn't "that kind" of officer. He had seen enough rules-and-regulation asshole brass in his life to turn him into an anarchist forever.

A bottle was thrown across to him, and Stone grabbed it from the air. He opened it with the hilt of his long, custom bowie, having found the exact spot that created identical torques and angles to a can opener, and took a deep swig.

He turned his head and spat it out, but surreptitiously, so the other men didn't see him and feel hurt by his rejection of their homemade brew. Excaliber, who had been lying with his head on his paws, sniffed the air, and his eyes grew alert. He rose up, stretching his back into a sudden hump and then back down again, and then moseyed the few feet over to Stone, who let the bottle dangle at his side.

"Want some dog?" Stone asked, holding the amber bottle up to the pitbull's mouth. The fighting dog had enjoyed Dr. Kennedy's brew—maybe he'd like this. The huge sandpaper-like tongue darted out like a snake's as Stone poured a little of the foaming liquid onto it. Excaliber slurped it back in, paused a second while the taste buds and like-dislike judgment centers of his brain argued things out for a moment. The "like" clearly won as the dog shot back to the bottle and his tongue lapped in and out quickly over and over again like some kind of pink suction device. Stone poured a steady stream of the brew out, and though half of it bounced off the slapping tongue, Excaliber quickly finished the bottle off. He stood back and burped, then turned unsteadily and headed back to where he had been and lay down again getting into nearly exactly the same position he had been minutes before. One eye closed, the other half open, his tongue hanging slightly out of his mouth like a flap out of a shoe, he looked all in all the picture of pitbull contentment.

Stone's mind was boiling. The responsibility of saving the whole damned state was on his back now. And he didn't like it. April too. He hadn't even thought about her for the last two days—he'd been too busy just surviving, just keeping the wolves at the door. He was just a mortal man. A *nadi*—yes, the term the Ute Indians had given him after they saved him from violent death. He with the gift of death. Yes, Stone had it, but he also had a heart and a gut. And they both felt like they were about to explode. From the moment he had left his father's mountain bunker, Stone had been fighting. And though so far he had won them all, the battles had gotten bigger each time, the stakes higher. It was as if he were rising in some kind of hierarchy of war. Some unknown battle plan taking him somewhere he couldn't even begin to imagine.

"April, April," Stone sent out from his trembling mind into the star-riddled sky above, flashing with meteors, slivers of light that slashed across the black and blue skies like swords leaving long, ethereal trails in their wake. "I've got to do one thing first. But I swear I'll get you. Hang on, baby. Hang on." He did something he hadn't done for years, and he felt like a fool as he did it. But pulling a blanket up over his chest as he lay, head back against his rolled-up jacket, Stone put his hands together in prayer, closed his eyes, and asked whoever ran this sick show to give his sister a break. To let her live. And if she had to die—if it was her time—to not let her get raped or mutilated. But just take her—fast. With a bullet or a bomb.

When he awoke with a start the next morning, Stone heard something growling at his feet and discovered his hands still clenched tightly against each other, his teeth sore from having ground against each other throughout the chilly night. His eyes opened, and he saw the pitbull about three feet directly in front of his face. It was staring straight down at something right in front of Stone. He looked sleepily down, raising one hand to rub his swollen eye and froze in the air. A rattler! A big son of a bitch too. This one looked to be six feet long. It was coiled back not two feet from Stone's shoulder, coiled like a spring, its head balanced up on its swaying body, tongue snapping in and out. It stared at both of them, unsure of which was the more dangerous, and flicked its eyes back and forth, trying to keep both of them at an equal distance.

Stone was in no position to move fast, his entire weight on his side where he had been sleeping. But the serpent seemed more concerned about the growls coming from the pitbull and the incisors that glistened in the rays of the morning sun. The snake had probably been slithering by after night hunting, and Excaliber had seen it. It would have been better just to let it go by. But then, growing pitbulls had to have their fun. Stone stayed absolutely still, as if he were a statue. Excaliber's head suddenly moved fast from the right, and the snake launched itself right up into the air, its jaws opened wide, fangs dripping with poisonous venom. But the pitbull's charge had been just a feint. As quickly as it started from the right, the dog twisted his back and around like a Slinkie, and came in from the left. The timber rattler sensed the change in direction at the last second, but it was too late. It had already launched—and there was no turning back.

The entire length of the black-and-gray diamond-patterned snake seemed for an instant to spread straight out as its fangs closed on the spot that the pitbull had just been inhabiting. But the canine jaws ripped up from underneath, coming into the thing sideways. His teeth closed cleanly around the head, and he bit hard. Then just as quickly he opened the white mouth and spat out again, and the snake flew off in pieces. Stone pulled himself out of the way of the whipping, but now harmless, body of the thing that fell across his shoulder. With disgust he ripped it free and flung it off and then glanced down at the ground where the head and but a few inches of the body still writhed around, the jaws still opening and closing. Excaliber slapped his paw against the thing, and damned if it didn't try to bite him. But with nothing to propel itself, the dying animal jawed feebly at the air like an old man without his dentures.

Stone rose, threw his boots on, and crushed the wretched leftover, putting it out of its misery. He patted the pitbull on the head. "Owe you again, dog, even though I suspect you had something to do with the whole event." Excaliber looked up at him with supreme innocence. Stone got the whole crew up, and after a quick few pots of coffee, boiled on little stoves inside the tanks, they were on the road again. Stone went slowly at first, not sure they would actually remember the lessons of yesterday. But behind him the two tanks steered as straight and steady as a ruler. He added five miles per hour every fifteen minutes or so. Within a few hours they were cruising north across a crumbling interstate highway cutting up through the mountains at thirty-plus.

The day was clear, the sun burning down through an almost cloudless sky, and as they rose up into the Rockies the peaks around them took on an almost mystical beauty, mountains shimmering with snowcapped crowns; blankets of pine trees, every branch frosted with a million jewels of ice. Above them, hawks circled, lazily searching for the movement of a rabbit or a groundhog far below. And after a half hour of climbing, Stone, looking from inside the tank with the scanning video camera, could see down into chasms thousands of feet deep. If one of the tanks went over there, there'd be no need of a rescue mission. There's a silver lining in every cloud—no matter how bloody it may be.

They reached the summit of this particular set of low mountains in the eight- to ten-thousand foot range and started back down the other side. Stone scanned ahead to the north as they descended. He could see miles off, lowlands stretching to the horizon, more treed than the terrain they had just been through. Stone had already formulated a plan —and that was a plan for what to do when he hadn't a fucking idea of what to do. Go to the bunker.

The bunker—carved into the side of a mountain at the northern edge of Estes National Park in northern Colorado. There Stone had lived for five years with his father, the Major; and his mother and his sister, April. One big happy family screaming at each other, staying out of each other's way. But now the Major was dead, his mother raped and killed, and April... The Major had installed a complex computer system in the place and had been storing up data for years in the damned thing.

Maybe there was information there that could be useful. He had to start somehow, and as they were within thirty miles of the place according to his calculations, Stone couldn't see that it would hurt. Also, although he wouldn't even really admit it to himself, Stone hoped that somehow April had been able to make it there and was waiting for him.

They reached the bottom of the mini range and another flat landscape and had been traveling on it for several minutes when Stone glanced away from the front-angle drive screen and up to the 360-degree scan monitor. He dropped his eyes back down and then ripped them up again, doing a double take. At the eastern and western flanks, at the very edges of the screen, he swore he saw vehicles. He slowed the Bradley slightly, whispering "Drop five" into the mouth mike, meaning slow down five miles per hour. He kept his eyes on the 360 screen and leaned forward anxiously. Yes, there was something. There were—

"Jesus fucking Christ," Stone blurted out as his eyes took in what was being transmitted back by the rotating camera. They were surrounded on both flanks by dozens of bizarre vehicles, streaming down the sides of two hills. And bizarre wasn't even the word to describe them. There wasn't a word. Wooden, boxlike frames had been built over truck and car chassis. The things were like raw machines, all the gears and workings exposed, smoke pouring from every crack. Some had what looked like crow's nests, towers of wood that swayed back and forth in the air as the primitive vehicles below them charged. They were loaded down on all sides with savage-looking fellows, with long beards and manes of greasy hair. Every one of them carried some sort of blunderbuss. And they were headed straight toward the tanks.

"Defensive formation!" Stone screamed into the mouthpiece. He had had time to go over some of the battle strategies he had picked up from both Patton and the Major's computer the last time he had been there. He wasn't a genius to say the least, but a tank was a formidable weapon, so if he just didn't fuck things up . . . He saw that the way ahead was blocked; the mountain men had created a small avalanche some four hundred feet ahead. He didn't want to get stuck with his back to them. The three tanks wheeled around and came to a stop, creating a three-pointed star with the long muzzles of their cannon protecting each side.

"Just open up," Stone shouted, "with everything you got. And don't stop until I give the command." He slammed back into his seat, put his hands over the firing triggers of both the 50-cal machine gun and the immense 120-mm cannon. The tank slammed back on its treads, throwing Excaliber to the floor from a warm shelf he had discovered above the exhaust pipe. He immediately sent out a growl of disapproval. The shell tore into the left slope, landing almost directly between two trucklike vehicles with high steel sides and double-thick tires. The dirt erupted up in orange and red flames, but when the dust settled, both were still heading right toward the encircled wagon train of high-tech battle wagons.

"Son of a fucking bitch," Stone cursed under his breath. That wasn't the way it was supposed to happen. These assholes were supposed to go out fast from a 120-mm. He could see the other tanks shooting out their huge shells as two thunderous roars erupted on each side of him. Stone followed by watching the 360 video sweep, which was on double time now, so the entire surroundings were flashed to Stone every 2.5 seconds. It was hard not to get dizzy. One of them slammed into a VW minibus from which the whole top had been ripped and filled with seats in which the dirt-coated attackers sat so they could fire in comfort. This particular batch took the direct blast at about the center of the "bus," and bodies went flying every which way. The other shell came down just in front of an old Dodge with a machine gun mounted on top and sent that, too, careening up into the air, as if it were trying to get into orbit, the machine gunner spiraling off in a different direction until his skull met the side of a boulder and painted it red. The Dodge, with its engine dripping out the front, came crashing down just in front of a speeding biker who slammed into it head-on. Then the whole thing erupted as leaking gasoline from the car ignited.

But others poured through the wall of flame. Rifle and pistol fire was coming from every car, and as Stone glanced to the top of a monitor, he saw that more was coming every second. He could hear the slugs pinging off the armor of the tank, sharp little sounds that reverberated through the tank. He fired again, trying to sight up one of the command cars that was now coming dead on toward them only a few hundred feet off. The tank reeled back, and the huge shell flew out of the smoking barrel just feet above the ground. It missed the target Stone had aimed for—the lead car—with someone who must have been closely related to Genghis Khan standing on the hood, firing some kind of rocket grenade. But the shell streamed past the gang leader and slammed into the front end of a diesel truck cab. The front end disintegrated as if the hammer of Thor had descended from the heavens.

Stone saw the war-painted man—in blood as far as Stone could tell through the video monitor—fire the long, tubular device he was carrying. Some sort of shell rocketed toward the Bradley and slammed right into its side, just a yard away from Stone. The entire tank shook, and every one of them, including Excaliber, went flying around the interior. Stone gripped the seat with both hands. In a second the tank settled and he could feel the heat of the explosion coming right through the titanium-armored wall.

Things weren't quite working out as he had hoped. The tanks were tough, but they couldn't just let themselves stand there taking all the assorted slugs, grenades, and mini-rockets these blood-smeared mountain thuds could dish out. Stone sighted up on the bastard who was slamming another load into his launcher. The vehicles were streaming down from everywhere now, a solid sheet of them—rusted hulks with coughing engines, absolutely loaded with blood-coated men firing constantly. Again Stone missed what he had sighted, but the shell landed dead on through the windshield of an ancient Ford, wide tail fins and all. The man's head disappeared inside, as did the entire car a second later, exploding out a curtain of steel and glass, slicing myriad cuts into men hanging on to the charging vehicles around it.

One of the truck bodies from which the whole back had been stripped off, and a single high crow's nest built up on it, suddenly caught Stone's attention. The plywood cabin in the sky, a good twenty feet up, the foot-thick pole beneath it wired down to all four sides, glistened for a second with the reflection of steel, and Stone saw a small cannon muzzle poking through an opening. The bastards even had artillery. The thing roared, and the entire pole seemed to lean backward. Stone heard a blast to the right of him, and as the camera panned by, he saw that Bull's tank was enveloped in flame. Phosphorus bomb.

"Don't panic," Stone yelled into the mouthpiece, as he heard screams of raw terror coming over his headset from inside the blazing tank. "Listen to me, you bastards," Stone shouted at the top of his lungs. "You're self-contained in there. The flames can't get to you—I swear to God. Bull, flip the 'Internal Oxygen' switch on the panel in front of you. You hear me, do it fast!"

"Can't—breathe," a voice whispered back. "Can't—"

"The switch, the switch. Oxygen on!"

"Yeah, I see it. There." Then the voice died out. Shit, the specs said the Bradley could easily take a hit like that. But the specs had been wrong before, many times. If a whole tankload of them died already . . . The video scanned past the burning tank, and Stone saw that the flames were already dying down, but suddenly Foster was emerging from the top. The idiot had panicked and opened the hatchway. He closed it, or someone did from below, and the terrified man ran to the edge of the tank to jump down. He had barely started his descent when slugs tore into him from every direction. A hundred rounds must have ripped into the flesh within two seconds, and the body spun and jerked wildly in the air, held in place momentarily by the sheer force of the multitude of bullets. Then the flood of lead ceased, and the body, bleeding from so many holes that it would take an hour or two to count them all, slammed down onto the dust and flopped around like a spastic worm.

This couldn't go on, Stone suddenly realized. If he had an ace in the hole, it was time to use it—or there wouldn't be any more games to be played. He slammed his hand down on the "Missile Systems On" button, and a whole portion of the control panel suddenly lit up.

"Missiles?" The machine read out on the computer terminal before him.

"All." Stone slammed his finger down on the answering button.

"Range?"

"Impact detonation," Stone input. "Firing at ninety degrees."

"Formation?" the missile systems computer program asked.

"Four left, four right," Stone input. He glanced up at the video screen and saw that the vehicles were almost upon them. Once there, they could plant dynamite, petrol bombs. It was now or—

"Systems armed," the screen read out. "Signal launch to implement."

Stone ground his thumb down hard onto the "Launch" button. There was a whirring sound, and above them, the top of the tank seemed to lift up, at least to those killers who were within yards of the Bradley, bringing their vehicles to a screeching stop. On each side of the turret a missile rack popped up into view, four steel tubes with the tips of shining, cone-shaped noses just poking out of them. The things buzzed and clicked and quickly spun around into firing position, moving on ball bearings hidden in the armor below. They seemed to set themselves, as if shocks were coming out beneath them, and then they fired.

The leader of this particular group of slime, who had fired the grenade launcher at Stone's tank, had just driven up to the side of the Bradley as the missiles went off. In fact, he was looking right at the point of one, reaching his hand out to touch it. It took his head clean off as it shot free of its launching pad—severing the tattooed face cleanly from its body—but not detonating, as the flesh didn't even offer enough resistance to its sensing devices to trigger it. On each side of Stone's tank, four Mini-Hawks, the most powerful short-range missile ever built, shot out exactly six feet above the ground, their own computer-guidance systems taking control. They began veering off from one another within a fiftieth of a second, heading left and right. By the time they reached the first lines of the advancing cars and trucks ahead, they were about thirty feet apart.

Eight mountains of fire erupted around the three besieged tanks. The very ground beneath them seemed to shake, and the Bradleys shook back and forth, buffeted from every side by shock waves. It took almost twenty seconds for the main explosion to settle down and just the secondaries to continue on, little pops here and there through the thick tank walls. Stone's brain ceased ringing like a bell. He wondered if the video camera mounted topside was still functioning, but as he raised his eyes to the screen he saw that it was. And the scene it transmitted back was one of total devastation. The attack vehicles lay strewn every which way, steel bodies peeled back like opened tuna-fish cans, melted tires like gumdrops too long in the sun. And the bodies—or pieces of bodies, really—lay draped over everything, like the final strokes of a painting, buckets of blood and ground-up flesh heaved over the picture, adding a certain element of unquestionable finality.

Here and there Stone could see bodies moving feebly through the smoke, as the vehicles burned like bonfires on both slopes, like some sort of sacred ceremony of winter. Ceremony of death. The invasion was clearly over.

"Let's move out," Stone said over the mike as he guided his Bradley over the wreckage and toward the boulder barricade. He lowered the huge 120-mm and began firing from a hundred yards off and kept firing, so that by the time they reached it, the wall had been pulverized and the three tanks were easily able to mount the debris with their thick climbing treads.

Behind them, those mountain bandits who were left, those who could still move, gathered what was left of their gang and the two or three vehicles that still functioned and started heading slowly back to their mountain hideout. Many of the living were without hands, arms, legs. They would have to lay low for a while, pull back some of their operations, hide, heal their wounds. But for this particular band of cutthroats, murderers, rapists, and mutilators, though they couldn't admit it to themselves, their backs were broken. They would never rule the mountains again. They had been destroyed.

CHAPTER

EIGHT

T HERE'S SOMETHING about killing that makes a man hungry. Maybe it makes him feel his own mortality and want to fill up on as much chow as possible in case he is suddenly called to the great beyond. After all, who knows what's to eat up or down there? Or how long a trip it is. Suffice it to say that when they stopped about four hours later after traveling nonstop on an almost perfectly northerly direction on the compass, the men were ravenous and lit into the food that Hartstein, who was turning out to be a pretty good cook, threw together from a deer that he had his gunner shoot with his 50-cal during the journey. He'd jumped down from the tank, slit its throat and chest to bleed the son of a bitch, and then had just let it sort things out on the back of the Bradley for the next few hours. There wasn't a huge amount of the big buck left after the 50s had done their work, but there was enough for nine men and a dog.

Which was fine with Stone. He wanted them to all be

stuffed, too tired even to think. For he was close enough to the bunker now to check a few things out. He had three of them help him unhitch the Harley from the back of the Bradley and saw that it had taken a few shots in the body. But no lines or electrical connections had been severed, and the bike looked functional. Posting two guards, Stone told them he had to check out something ahead and would be back in several hours. They looked bored and waved him and Excaliber off as they roasted more strips of the meat. The pitbull was torn between the sizzling juices of the buck and accompanying Stone. But he knew instinctively that they were near the bunker and that somehow it was important for him to go with Stone. It was, after all, a fighting dog's responsibility to be with his master at all major battles, wars, and reconnaissances. Or so Excaliber and his breed had always felt, since their warrior bloodline had been bred into their existence. Besides, there were a few foods that the bullterrier remembered from the bunker that it wouldn't mind trying again. Already it was trying to plot some way of getting Stone to give it some treats.

Things were going better with the crew than Stone could have hoped. But that only gave him a chance to worry about other things—about April. She hovered in his mind like a ghost, an accusing presence that said nothing but stared at him with big, helpless eyes. And always blood, blood spouting from her; from her face, her fingertips.

The Harley flew through the frigid night, its sharp beam lighting up the darkness ahead. The woods on all sides of him grew still, menacing, with shadows suddenly dancing around as they were created and stirred up by the passing light of the motorcycle. The dog growled beneath its breath as it stared off into a grove of trees. Stone twisted the accelerator a little harder. He knew the animal was seeing something, sensing something, that humans couldn't. Something that wasn't friendly waiting out in those woods.

But soon they were heading along the rising mountain

road that led to the hideaway. Stone knew it had cost the Major nearly a million, maybe more, to build that place. It had been blasted and carved right into the side of a mountain that his family had owned, along with hundreds of acres, just north of Estes National Park. His father had started saying ten years ago that nuclear war was coming, that the country would collapse. And Stone had thought him a right-wing fool, an ex-Ranger and millionaire weapons-manufacturer who believed his own propaganda. He and the Major had fought over so many things in their years together, both outside and inside the bunker.

Five years they had been in there. Five years. It seemed impossible, a meaningless number. Five years of his mother and father and sister all living inside walls, in a twenty-thousand-square-foot space equipped with all the most modern conveniences—kitchen; sauna; immense living room; separate bedrooms and living quarters; a war room filled with weapons and ammunition; experimental quarters, including Stone's father's computer center; and a firing range built in the back of the bunker, hacked out of the solid granite walls. Stone had hacked them a lot deeper during their firing sessions over five years. As much as Stone had resented the old man, in many ways he had come to see that the Major had been right about a lot of things. He had swallowed his pride and allowed his father to teach him. So for the first time, inside the confines of the world's costliest fallout shelter, Major Clayton R. Stone had taught his son, Martin, all the tricks in the book—and those that weren't, as well. His father had been the last of a tough, tough breed. The last of the Rangers—the ultra-special forces of the U.S. military services. And now he was gone. But somehow what he knew, and had stood for, lived on in Martin Stone. Whether Martin wanted it or not, he had been handed the mantle. He had been chosen to be the Last Ranger.

"Thanks, Dad," Stone spat out into the night air, which had now turned to an inky blackness as the stars and moon struggled to punch their way through the layers of clouds that drifted above the mountains. Stone grimaced as he hunched down lower on the bike to protect his lips and face from the now freezing winds. Excaliber sank down behind him, spreading all four legs around the leather seat like a starfish around a clam and hanging on with every bit of muscle power he could exert, which with a pitbull is enough to require a crane to extract him. Excaliber burped loudly behind him, snapping Stone's mind from his moody wanderings. The dumb dog was always pulling him from depression. "Dog, what did I do before I met you?" Stone laughed into the night air, turning his head for a second. Excaliber sniffed back and let out a loud fart, then another, then a whole series. Though the bike was moving at about forty miles per hour, the wind streaming past Stone's face to the back, he still got a whiff of the remains of the pitbull's overindulgence in buck dinner and wished he hadn't.

"Jesus stinking Christ," Stone yelled, turning again. "Keep your ass pointed south, dog—you hear me? I'm going to have to start feeding you Tums and Pepto-Bismol." Although just where he could obtain either of those items in the barbarous, collapsed civilization that was now America was a little beyond him. But after a whole series of putts, burps, and little grunts of exertion, the dog suddenly spat up a well-browned eyeball of the mountain elk that he had gobbled down too fast. After the ejection of the eye, which Stone had the fortune not to witness or he might well have lost much of his dinner as well, the terrier settled down once again, trying to lie on its side, as its distended stomach felt hot and boiling with gas. It tried to remind itself not to eat so much or so fast the next time. But it knew as it did so that it would forget, and in fact immediately did forget, as it started remembering the last time they had been to the bunker and the master had opened cans. There had been many cans, filled with delicious things. Its eyes half closed as it saw visions of dog delicacies floating by like little clouds just above its head.

Stone grew wary as they approached the last stretch of main road that led to the bunker. It was a long stretch of cracked highway that had been snow-covered the last time he had been through. He had been attacked by two mountain men on snowmobiles and had taken them out before they took him, but it had been close. He eyed the almost flat road ahead, suddenly lit up by the Harley's beam, and accelerated sharply—just in case. Within seconds he had the bike up to fifty, then sixty and seventy. The road was firm, hard-packed, and the evening clear, so with the long, tungsten-filtered headlight he could see for hundreds of yards. The Harley tore along like a racehorse, beautiful, sleek, its streamlined weaponry poking off it like quills ready to stab out. As the bike roared along Stone suddenly saw flashes of light from the woods on the right. Attack. He twisted the accelerator even further, and the motorcycle shot into over-drive, accelerating almost effortlessly to a hundred miles per hour. It tore along, almost impossible to see, as the slugs fired by the thirty or so half-retarded mountain boys with no teeth and heads that came to little points didn't come near the bike but just whistled by in its airstream.

Stone didn't stop until he had reached the start of the mountain road, fourteen miles on. Then he slowed the bike to a crawl and edged it between a wall of dense bush, hanging vines, and branches. Thorns and twigs scratched against his skin, and Excaliber barked as an ear got pierced by a particularly long needle. But at last they were through and onto the deer path that weaved and rambled all over the place to the bunker. His father had planned for it to be this isolated from the very start. There was no reason for anyone to have any idea that something was up this way. It had been left as undeveloped as it had been before the place was built, even to the extreme of using special wheeled trucks up to the deer path and then three-wheeled vehicles the rest of the way. And from the lack of a trace of any tire tracks other than a few indentations of the Harley's wheels left the last time he was here, it was working. No one had come by.

Soon the sheer rock face behind which the bunker had been built loomed into view, and Stone brought the Harley to a slow stop. He stepped off, and the auto kickstand snapped into place, anchoring the still droning bike on wide alloy metal pads on the ground. Stone walked over to a table-sized boulder and pushed his shoulder against it hard. Either he was getting weaker or the damn thing had put on weight since the last time he had come. But at last it budged slightly and then started shifting away. The hole that it covered was revealed, and Stone reached down into it and grabbed hold of a plastic bag at the bottom. He extracted a small transmitter from the bag and, aiming it at the solid rock wall, pressed the device.

The mountainside made a sound and then seemed to split in two as the rock face, for a height of ten feet, slid apart in two pieces. They moved silently all the way to each side until a large rectangular opening big enough to drive a truck into had been created. Stone remounted the Harley and eased it inside, using both feet on the ground to guide it. Once inside, he dismounted again and headed into the innards of the bunker. The three-foot-thick rock walls slid closed again with just a hiss of compressed air. Then all was quiet again.

It always felt strange for him to come into this place—their presence was so strong. He could see them, hear them talking, arguing, laughing. It gave Stone an eerie feeling, yet at the same time a secure one, to be here. This, for better or worse, was all the home he had. It was the only place he really felt safe. Behind those granite walls he could at last totally relax, not even have to have a pistol or knife on hand at all times, as he did out there. So the first thing Stone did as he came into the living room—with its sunken multi-levels, its deep comfortable designer couches, and modern art on the walls—was take out his .44 Mag and his Uzi

9-mm automatic pistol and heave them on one of the couchs —the couch that had been officially his all those years. For they had each had their own space—their own allotted area. They'd had to or they would have gone mad. Every animal needs territory, even if it's measured in inches. The living area, which had been the Major's pride and joy, really was a beautiful space—high ceilings with indirect lighting from above so it almost gave the effect of daylight; expensive rugs; paintings on the walls; fish tanks, still bubbling happily away, fish fed automatically by computer, cleaned, oxygenated, every damned thing. The Major had spared no expense in making the place as nice as he could. Yes, let's all live happily after nuke war and the breakdown of civilization.

Stone took the thick, rolled-up canvas he had taken from the Harley and unrolled it on the floor. The Michelangelo— the painting of the Creation—that he had taken from the ruins of Patton's headquarters back at Fort Bradley. He stared at it as it lay on the floor, mesmerized by its beauty, its huge, sweeping clouds, its angles drifting down, and God's hand reaching down to strike life into mankind. Then, in a kind of trance, Stone took the wide canvas and nailed it up on the wall. He knew it was all insane—a gift of some kind for his family, for his father. A way, perhaps, of showing there had been love between them, when now there was really no way to show it. At least it would survive in here. Out there it would have been eaten, drenched with rain, gone to tatters within months.

Stone wanted nothing more than to take a shower, get in bed for about a year. But he couldn't leave the attack force alone for more than a few hours. He just didn't *trust* them. So he headed immediately for his father's computer room, not even allowing himself to lie down on the couch for one second, knowing he wouldn't get up for days. Wearily, he plodded down the hall, glancing behind him for Excaliber, but the pitbull had already disappeared into some hallway or other. The animal had been here before; it would find its way around. Stone reached the steel door that guarded the computer section and punched in the access code on a small digital keypad that rested in the wall. Within seconds the door slid and he walked inside the large, high-tech workshop. It still slightly boggled his mind that his father had installed all this stuff in here. Stone hadn't come into the room the entire five years he had lived in the bunker. Only after the Major had died of a sudden heart attack had he entered.

Lights and meters, readout monitors, screens, graphs, all beeped and flashed throughout the room. Apparatus was piled atop apparatus, so that the place looked like a madman's junk shop. Only it wasn't junk but all the latest high-tech gear—in computers, computer linkups, data gathering. His father had brought in tons of computer parts and backups when he had stocked the place. And everything still seemed to work perfectly. Stone knew as he moved among them that the machines were automatically carrying out all sorts of tasks—from measuring the radiation in the air outside to attending to the bunker's life-support systems, temperature controls, solar panel adjustments. . . . The computer system ran the whole fucking show.

Stone sat down at the main work substation and flicked the monitor and keyboard on. The thing roared to life with a whir, and several little green lights came on here and there around the machine. The thing was user-friendly, thank God, and a menu suddenly appeared on the screen in little green letters, asking him the category of information he wanted access to.

"Great," Stone muttered to himself as he faced the screen. This was always the problem—what question to ask the fucking thing. He had no idea how much information his father had had access to or been able to process into the system. It would just have to be trial and error.

"Missile Sites," Stone punched into the keyboard before

him. The machine clicked, and a few lights went on and off as it communicated with the mainframe off on the other side of the room, a large box, a simplified version of a Cray II, one of the most advanced computer systems. But the thing beeped a few times, a red warning light flashed on and off, and then a message flashed on the screen. A message from the dead, from his father.

"Martin, I can only assume if you are reading this that I am dead and that for some reason you must have access to this information. In the last few months before it all came down, I was able to tap into a number of military computer systems for the whole central portion of the country—and gather quite a bit of information. Also, as the U.S. deteriorated, there was still a lot of transmissions going on via satellite from one isolated installation to another. This, too, was fed into the mainframe. Thus you will discover there is a wealth of material for you to draw from. Merely key in your subject by name, and the Cray will either display this information or help you find it—if this is possible."

Stone watched the streams of letters as they fed across the screen in front of him. The hand of his father had input all this. It was weird, as if the old man were still sitting in this chair, as if his ghost danced among the circuitry. Stone felt a shudder ripple through his body, and he tried to concentrate on the screen—keep the rest out.

"But first, just to make sure no one else has gained access to this computer, you must answer a question that no one else could know, but you, I, and your mother. That is the access code to this part of the computer's classified information. It's silly, but I couldn't think of another one as good."

"Come on, Dad, come on," Stone said impatiently. He'd been away from the tank force three hours already and hadn't even begun to get anything together. But the question flashed on the screen, and Stone's face wrinkled up in a wide smile.

"What was the name of your pet hamster when you were

twelve, the one that died of a heart attack during a thunderstorm?" Stone stared at the screen, numerous emotions rippling across his face. Because for the life of him he couldn't remember. So much had happened recently that many memories of his old life were in shambles, drifting tatters of thought; broken images that he could hardly remember and didn't know for sure if they were real or just dreams. The hamster—what the fuck was its name? The blank space after the flashing cursor on the screen waited for him to fill it in, and Stone started madly typing names.

"Clifton, Spike, Charlie, Ink, Topper..." Every name he could vaguely remember liking when young. But the computer rejected them all, one after another, flashing a red light and the words "Incorrect Answer" each time. This was ridiculous. The fate of Colorado itself hanging on his long dead pet hamster. "Aquaman," he suddenly typed impulsively into the keyboard, remembering that the underwater hero had been a particular favorite of his and he had collected hundreds of the comic books.

The screen clicked, whirred, and a green light went on above it, then the words "You may proceed" appeared.

"Missile Sites," Stone punched in again, slamming the "Command Execute" button.

"Location?" the computer asked.

"Utah, Colorado area." Stone keyed in. The thing whirred again, and across the room Stone heard the mainframe itself switch into gear as lights lit up along one side of the steel square the size of a large refrigerator into and out of which wires ran all over the place, connecting the central portion of the computer system to all the other functions it carried out throughout the bunker. Within about twenty seconds a list of nearly fifty locations appeared on the screen. Stone whistled. Great. Suddenly the computer terminal started spouting out more data.

"Nonfunctional, forty-seven—functional three. Locations —Livermore, Wellington, Pawnee. Of remaining three, transmission monitored by radioscan, indicate, Livermore and Wellington are functional and active." A map appeared at the top of the screen as the image split into two, showing a map of northern Colorado. The two locations flashed green, on and off, right next to each other, only fifty or so miles north of where Stone was standing. "Each silo known to contain one ten-megaton ICBM missile, capable of ten-thousand-mile flight path. Two man firing crew, requiring simultaneous double key turn for execution of firing commands." The message stopped, and a question mark appeared, asking him what further information he required.

Stone's jaw hung open as he stared at the screen. He had thought at best it might give him a vague clue as to where to proceed, but it had pinpointed it exactly. And suddenly Stone remembered Patton mentioning the word *Livermore* over the radio back at Fort Bradley when they had been on better terms. Stone hit the "Close-up" button, and the map suddenly enlarged a hundred times, bringing the local detail of the terrain into superlarge perspective so Stone could see every road, every mountain, for ten miles around the place. He pressed "Close-up" again, and the image inside the screen seemed to rush up at him as if he were falling from a plane getting nearer and nearer to its very microscopic surface. A detailed plan of the silo itself filled the screen, showing levels, entrances, control booth. . . .

Stone studied the information for several minutes and then cleared the screen, starting from scratch. This time he keyed in "Personnel."

In a few seconds the computer asked, "Service, name, rank?"

"Army, General Patton III," Stone keyed in, and sat back with his chin in his hand, wondering if it would even have a thing on him.

The mainframe behind him chugged away, as if it were struggling with the question. After about thirty seconds the reply came. "No record of General Patton III on normal service personnel files; however, standard cross-reference check to radioscan shows mention of such a name as commander of the New American Army. Cross-check shows man previously to have been identified as Colonel Strath. Records as follows." The computer proceeded to read out line after line of Patton née Strath's biography: Education at West Point; Distinguished army career; Service in Vietnam, and as a colonel just before the country collapsed. It all looked innocuous enough, Stone thought as he rested his head down on both folded elbows and watched the lines scroll by one after another.

Then it came to "Psychiatric Evaluation," and Stone's eyes opened wide. "Manic depressive, with delusions of grandeur—bordering on psychosis." Stone read, fascinated, as what were apparently a number of detailed psychiatric reports scrolled by him. The Führer had had quite a few problems along the way. But his good-old-boy buddies in the higher echelons with whom he trained with at the Point had kept him out of trouble. The man obviously was mad. He had paranoid delusions that he was meant to be a great savior to mankind and that others were out to stop him. He would do anything "that had to be done" to take them out. But apparently he had been put on some sort of medication, and the whole thing had been swept under the carpet.

Yeah, only now he ain't taking his medication no more, Stone thought with disgust as he got to the end of the readout. The monitor went back to a blank screen to await his next request. Stone fed some more questions about tank warfare into the computer. Questions about flanking, strategies for armor against armor, the advantage of mobile over stationary tactics. Every bit of information he could get his hands on. He was about to try to take on what was probably the most powerful and well-armed force in the country. With three tanks. Stone just kept wishing he could lie down, could just fall into endless sleep. Because nothing he was finding out was making him feel any more fucking cheerful. He shut off the terminal, though the rest of the room kept humming away, a factory of information processing. He walked through the door. It slid closed behind him, the lights inside instantly shutting off. After all, computers didn't need light to see by. They had eyes inside their heads.

CHAPTER

NINE

STONE STARTED down the hall, his shoulders slumped, his head bowed forward. He felt in a daze, asleep on his feet, as if he hardly knew where he was. Shit, he just needed to sit down. Have a cup of coffee. Just ten minutes of nothing. There was too much information for his brain to process, to assimilate. Yeah, he'd just go in the kitchen and—

A blow slammed into the back of his skull, and his senses reeled. He felt himself falling into blackness as stars of brilliant color danced rapidly by before him. Then he felt his face slam into the wall, and though the blow was incredibly painful, pushing his nose in almost flat, the sheer electricity of its painfulness brought him out of near unconsciousness. He curled up into a ball at the base of the wall and spun around, pulling himself a foot to the side as he did so. And just barely in time, for the wall where his flesh had just been was stabbed by a long knife, the blade so strong and thick it pierced the plasterboard to the hilt. In the dim light of the long hallway with the soft, plush, low-cut carpeting beneath him, Stone could see there were four of them. How in hell they had gotten in here and how they even knew where the place was were questions that raced through his mind.

But for the moment he was more interested in the knives they all held, long stilleto-shaped commando blades, razor-sharp, with only one purpose—to kill human beings. They wore NAA camouflage slacks and black sweatshirts and jackets. And pinned to the lapels of each jacket, Patton's elite forces symbol—crossed fists over M16, the cheerful symbol of the Gestapo of the madman's army. They sneered at Stone, their faces all blackened with grease—their hands, too—so that not a patch of them would reflect any light. And this was the night he had decided to relieve himself of his weapons at the door, wanting to relax without their death dealing responsibility on his hip and shoulder every second of every day. And now . . . He promised himself that if he lived through all this, he would never take off his fucking guns again—even when he went to take a crap.

"Heard you were tough, tough boy," one of them said with a sneer as he came at Stone, slowly, one carefully placed foot at a time. "I think you're just dead meat." The man leapt forward, slashing down with the twelve-inch blade of the commando knife. Had it been anyone else but Martin Stone, the victim undoubtedly would have been rump roast. But Stone had trained for years in hand-to-hand and knife fighting. He had learned from the best, the very best. For the Major had been famous throughout Asia for his knife and other silent killing techniques. The severed heads of VC search-and-destroy forces sitting on poles along the Northern Mekong would attest to that. Stone, staying down low near the ground, was in excellent position to throw a low kick. He snapped his foot straight out and smashed into the attacker's kneecap. The thick ball of bone shattered with a crack like a huge chicken bone, and the leg suddenly bent backward at a weird angle. As the man stumbled forward, losing his balance and toppling over onto his left side, Stone slid up the wall he had been crouched against and caught the still outstretched knife hand in a strong grip. He twisted the hand up so the knife instantly fell free, and then helped the falling man on his journey by throwing his palm down behind the commando's neck and driving his face into the floor. Because it was carpet, it didn't crush his skull—it did smash everything in an inch or two, including his nose, which drove up into his skull. The nasal cartilage pierced right into the brain tissue and the man started, and then instantly stopped, a scream, a scream that caught in his throat as the engine that drove the whole fleshy deal stopped dead in its tracks.

But there was another assassin just behind him. The burly commando raised his knife in a lunging attack, slashing forward, and then back and forth, in a windmill of cuts. But Stone stepped back, once, twice, as the man took two steps forward. Then, as he started on a third, Stone rushed in, caught the swinging arm at the elbow, and pushed the knife past him, turning the attacker so that his side was exposed. Stone drove his own blade up and right through the rib cage, pushing it sideways—so it didn't catch on the bone, as his father had shown him—and deep into the attacker's flesh. The blade first pierced the man's lung, then his heart, cutting the aorta so that blood exploded out and all over Stone as well as the rug and walls. Stone ripped the knife out and pushed the man down the hall toward the two attackers as the dying NAA'er screamed out in pain, his hands slapped over the gushing fountain that poured from his side.

Stone took a chance. If he could just get to the other room and his pistols. He turned and started running. Never had the forty-foot-long hallway seemed so long or so dark. Like a child's nightmare, he just couldn't seem to get to the other end no matter how fast he ran. He was almost there when suddenly he felt something wrap around his feet and he fell forward, nearly slamming into the wall but deflecting himself with his raised arms. Still, he crashed down onto the carpeted floor and stared down at his feet where some sort of bololike device—two pieces of perfectly round steel attached to each end of a long leather thong, had wrapped two or three times around his ankles. He was hog-tied, and the NAA death squad—the two who were still alive—were tearing ass down the hallway with blood in their eyes. Stone reached forward to try to undo his tangled legs, knowing there was no way in hell he would be able to do it in time. As far as he could see, he was about to die.

Excaliber, meanwhile, had moseyed off the moment he had entered the bunker. He remembered the place well, having explored it thoroughly on his last visit when he had laid down a scent trail to remind him of just where the best observation posts were. The trail also led directly to the kitchen. Now the pitbull was already exploding with food, and even the thought of more made it feel a little ill. But it had daydreamed about the kitchen here, and the feeding frenzy it had experienced the last time here. It was pulled forward by pure lust, pure desire to fulfill its dog dreams. And so, remembering where Stone had taken the dozens of cans down from, Excaliber pushed a chair over to a wall, climbed up on it, and opened the door with his paw. The shining cans inside were piled high, but the dog had no way of knowing what taste lay in what container. He reached up with his paw and knocked a few cans down from the top of each pile. They tumbled over him, some landing on his head, then falling down to the tiled kitchen floor. When it seemed like there was enough of a sampling—to start, anyway— the pitbull jumped back down and began nosing the cans around.

Paradise at its feet, the terrier sniffed at the metal containers, batted them with its paws, whined at them, did everything a dog could to persuade them to open and release their flavorful morsels. But nothing being forthcoming, the pitbull regressed to a more primitive approach, took one of the cans in his jaws, lifted it high, and snapped down hard on it. The incisors on both sides of his mouth pierced the can like a metal opener, and peach syrup began flowing through the holes. The dog balanced the can in its mouth and bit again, this time opening even larger holes so that some of the small half spheres of terribly sweet peaches squirted through and down into its mouth.

That was better. The pitbull shook the can back and forth, draining every bit of fluid and fleck of fruit inside. Then it flung the used receptacle aside, so it flew through the air and crashed at the far end of the kitchen. He sniffed around the pile of cans that lay strewn around and then poked at a big one, making it stand up on end. Opening his jaws to the maximum, the fighting terrier slammed them down hard, again piercing the container with four deep and even cuts. He lifted the can high in the air upside down and chomped again. This time pickles, gherkins and hamburger slices, mixed together, all flooded out and down into his throat. At first the dog liked the taste and gulped them down. But on the second gulp the thick, vinegary flavor made it cough, and the pitbull exploded in a violent sneeze, spitting the can halfway across the floor as small pickles of various shapes and sizes sprayed out, flying against drawers and tables around the entire kitchen.

Undaunted, after shaking its head a few times to clear its juice-flooded nose, the pitbull reached for another can and another. . . . It was draining the tenth can when it heard the first scream coming from the long hallway. The dog knew instantly that its master was in trouble, and it started across the smooth kitchen floor so rapidly that its claws scraped across the surface skidded in place. At last it got some friction going and shot forward, out of the kitchen and into the living room. It knew the direction instinctively and turned left at the living room, its back end skidding around and crashing over an aluminum light pole that lit one end of the room.

There, in the hall, the pitbull saw its master, and above

him were two men with pain things in their hands. The bull-terrier shot forward, this time getting good leverage against the carpeting of the hall. It accelerated like a rocket, coming out of nowhere before the two NAA commandos even saw it.

As the knife of one descended toward Stone's chest, the pitbull launched itself from about a yard behind its master. It flew straight over his shoulder and caught the falling hand at the wrist. The weight of the dog took the attacker right over on his side while the animal ground down hard with its rows of dagger teeth. As the assassin hit the floor Excaliber bit again and yanked hard—and the hand pulled free from the arm, dangling all kinds of spurting veins and tendons. The dog shook the thing a few times, the fingers slowly opening and closing in good-bye spasms, and then tossed it into the air so that it flew almost straight up, bounced off the ceiling, and came down just inches from the person who had previously owned it. The assassin screamed even louder when he saw the missing appendage.

As the second commando dived in for the kill, attempting to get at Stone, who was still extricating himself from the bolo around his ankles, Excaliber, knowing the first man was harmless, turned on a dime and again launched himself with tremendous speed toward the attacker. The man didn't even know what hit him. It could have been a meteor from space, so instantaneous and powerful was the blow. The pitbull's jaws came down square around the man's face. One second the commando could see Stone in front of him, and the next, just darkness and pain and the pink throat of a dog, for the pitbull had clamped its mouth over the front of the attacker's face, taking the whole thing between its jaws. The dog bit down hard, and the whole central portion of the elite fighter's face just sort of squashed together in a bloody mass. The pitbull ripped hard, and the man suddenly had no features—just a bloody pit out of which a scream emerged, the likes of which Stone had never heard before and hoped he never would again.

The faceless man fell to the carpet, blood pouring out of the holes that had once been his eyes, nose, cheeks. . . . For all was gone, just a huge wound, drenched in blood, a wound that pulsed as he screamed. Stone let his heart start slowing as he finally got himself extricated from the bolo device. He rose to his feet and called the dog, which was standing arrogantly between the two dying men like a hunter over its kills, daring either of them to rise again, to try anything. It glanced back and forth at them with a proud warrior stare and panted, its eyes wide with excitement.

"Here, boy," Stone said to call the animal, and it instantly trotted the few yards to him and stood by his side, rubbing its blood-soaked face against his leg. "You did good, dog. I'm going to see if I can't dig up some kind of medal or something."

Stone walked forward to see what remained of the attack force. The men in the back were all dead—the ones Stone had killed. The one with a missing hand appeared to be dead, or so near death that it hardly mattered—with ninety percent of his blood drained out of his body and all over the living room carpet within one minute.

The faceless man was the only one who was still alive somehow. And he shouldn't have been. Not the way he looked. No one who looked like that would want to live. Or so Stone thought as he walked up to the assassin, his hands over his face, as he rolled back and forth on the slippery red rug.

"Who told you I was here?" Stone asked the writhing figure. He didn't even know if the thing could speak, as its lips and teeth were gone—jaw too. But something uttered out of the red hole that moved where a mouth once might have been.

"You're traitor," the wound of a mouth gurgled, blood spewing out as it spoke. "We—we have a spy with you.

Have—" It tried to laugh, or act like it could, to impress Stone with its machismo. But it wasn't a good idea. Things spat up out of its throat, and blood seemed to just gush out of every opening of what had been a face.

"I'm going to do you a favor, asshole," Stone said, not particularly wanting to do what he was about to. He walked to the couch, picked up the .44 Mag sitting there, and then headed back to the hall. He held it out, muzzle pointing at the commando's heart. "I'm going to take you out of your pain, though God knows you wouldn't have done the same for me." Wincing a little, Stone pulled the trigger.

CHAPTER

TEN

I T TOOK Stone nearly an hour to make the place even vaguely presentable. He didn't know who he was making it presentable for, but he couldn't just leave blood and bodies lying all over the goddamn place. So he dragged them all outside about a quarter mile from the house to a pit they had used for compost and burning waste. He threw them in, poured two buckets of lye over them, and then covered the whole mess up with leaves and decay from another part of the heap. The bastards would at least help fertilize the ground, Stone couldn't help but think with a dark laugh. Daisies and dandelions would grow from their rotting remains. Recycled assassins.

At last he got things together and quickly gulped down three cups of black coffee to keep himself awake. He was so quickly supersaturated with the high-caffeine brew that his eyes were half popping from his head. Excaliber, now that the excitement was over, looked as sick as a dog. Though Stone could hardly believe it, he discovered that the animal had gone through numerous cans, just ripping them open, the shattered tins lying broken all over the syrup and juice-splattered floor. He couldn't even begin to get pissed off at the mutt after what it had just done. But when they were all mounted up on the Harley, Stone noticed that the dog was looking greener and greener around the gills. It had bitten off a little more here and there than it could chew. Stone headed out, closed the huge rock door behind them, and redeposited the "garage opener" back beneath the huge boulder so that if April came back, she could again have access to it. If, if, if . . .

Then he was on the bike and tearing down the dirt path as fast as the Harley could go without snagging into a tree. The pitbull looked more and more sick but clamped hold of the cool leather and closed his eyes, trying to pretend he was lying by a warm fire with a stomach about fifty percent smaller. The moon had sunk into the trees by the time Stone hit the bottom of the mountain path and got onto the main road. The Harley tore back along the long straightaway, Stone opening the big 1200-cc up to the limit, hitting a hundred and more when he was on flat patches of concrete and asphalt. Excaliber couldn't even look as the world sped by in a complete blur but buried his face deeper in the seat.

At last, as light just began to paint the far horizon with strokes of orange, Stone saw the cutoff that was the way back to the bivouacked tanks. He turned down a back road and then through some fields, slowing down as the going got rougher. As the sun poked the red pate of its burning head up over the trees, Stone saw the Bradleys silhouetted against some trees. The two guards greeted him as he came to a sputtering halt in front of them.

"Been hunting?" Ross asked him as he glanced down at Stone's jacket and pants. Stone looked down and saw that the entire lower portion of the uniform was streaked and mottled in red.

"Something like that," Stone replied, not wanting to tell

them what had really happened. There was a spy among them. It would be better for him not to reveal a thing—and perhaps the bastard would show himself. The men rose slowly as Stone yelled out, "Let's get this thing on the road." He was a wreck, and he knew it. He hadn't gotten any sleep, and God knows when he would again—maybe never. He could feel his eyes all puffed out, his lips dry and hot. Stone kept his eyes on each man as they rose from their blankets, searching among the eyes to see if any were shocked that he was there. But not one displayed the slightest double take or amazement. It gave Stone the creeps to walk among them and know that he had been set up by one of these sons of bitches.

Stone took over Hartstein's tank, switching crews and everything because he wanted access to another batch of the eight Mini-Hawk missiles that were hidden in the Bradley. Hartstein looked a little funny at him, but no one said a word. Stone knew that they all knew that he had used something extra—back there at the valley of burning cars. But he didn't offer any answers, and they didn't ask any questions. Stone was, after all, running this particular death show. Soon they were all inside, and Stone started the battle wagon up and headed straight north. The other two tanks fell in quickly behind him, and soon they were cruising along the relatively flat land between two ranges of mountains that moved in a north/south direction on each side of a five-mile-wide valley. Stone watched the two behind him, locking the video sweep on them for a while. But they hardly wavered at all. Both his choices had been good ones, for they were driving the things like they had been cruising around in the machines since high school. Gradually Stone opened up, until they were moving along at about forty miles per hour. The shock system of the Bradley was so well designed that the men inside were hardly aware that they were moving at that speed. It was more of a fluid motion, as if they were at sea, going over long swells. Even Excaliber seemed unperturbed and lay on the steel shelf above the exhaust piping, his front paws wiggling slightly as if he were running in his sleep.

They had been traveling at near maximum speed for about an hour, skirting between the two ranges when the gap of the valley suddenly opened and they were facing a wide plain that stretched off to the northern horizon. It looked blank and desolate, with just scraggly brush here and there, skinny cacti, tumbleweed blowing like pool balls across the hard ground. Stone slowed down some as he eased the tank onto the more granular surface than the stuff they had been on— just in case. The one thing he had learned so far was: Never take anything for granted. Even the ground you walk on. But the surface held good enough. Although covered with a loose, sandy surface, just inches beneath the top it was hard and firm, almost baked into a claylike substance, and the tanks easily found good traction.

They moved in a straight line like metal ducks following their mother, only these weren't so little, and their beaks had 120-meter firepower. Here and there, startled animals fled off into the prairie, their muscles flexing and uncoiling as their legs slammed into the earth to escape. They had gone but a few miles when Stone heard a low beeping and a red light to the right of the display panel was blinking. He glanced over.

"Radiation warning," the panel was reading out. "Tank is entering area of increasing radiation levels. The armoring of the Bradley is equipped to withstand 200 Rads/hour. Radiation Warning. Tank is entering . . ." Stone found the rad indicator and blanched. The thing was rising at the rate of about ten rads a minute. What the hell could—Stone flipped down the special long-range viewing system and set it on maximum focus. He peered into the periscopelike device and gasped. Now he knew why their fucking balls were being attacked by gamma rays. An immense crater from an atomic blast stood several miles ahead and to the left of the compass path they were following. Stone whistled as he eyed the thing, glancing at the road ahead, driving the Bradley with one hand.

The crater was immense. Like something from a dream—a bad, bad dream. It was nearly a mile wide and made of a reddish-brown dirt that rose perhaps half a mile into the sky with long, sloping sides that appeared almost smooth and glowing with just the hint of a green tinge throughout. It looked like something that should have been on the dark side of the moon, not down here on the planet Earth. It was as if the very soil of the planet had been twisted, melted together into this coagulated sculpture of destruction. As they got closer Stone saw just how ugly the thing was—and how deadly, for along its glasslike, sloping sides, carcasses were everywhere. Not from the initial blast that had just melted everything near it but from the radiation that had lingered. Animals that had wandered too close had actually touched its still superhot surface—were killed almost instantaneously. They literally ringed the base of the huge crater for a twenty-yard strip, thousands of them. Much of the hide and flesh on the animals—buffalo, elk, bear, groundhog, fox, wolf—was still attached to the creatures, as if they had hardly decayed at all. And as they drew closer and Stone peered through the greatly magnified image of the giant boil on the face of the earth, he saw that the dead were almost untouched, even their eyes still staring as if alive. It was the weirdest damned thing he had ever seen. As if they'd all been preserved, stuffed à la Tony Perkins' mother in *Psycho*.

Suddenly he realized what it was. The radiation. The same invisible energy that had killed the animals had also killed all the bugs, beetles, flies, even microscopic organisms, that usually fed off the dead. Thus everything that came to consume them tumbled to the crater's sloping wall instead and joined those who had already fallen. All living things die in the face of that much radiation. Thus they were all preserved in a never-never land of death with the appearance of life.

Stone checked the radiation meter and saw that it was passing two hundred rads. He was steering the column now at an angle away from the crater, but they couldn't get too far to the east or they'd run into a series of impassable chasms and fissures that, according to the tank's map system, were just miles off. So the men of the three-tank attack force gritted their teeth, for they could all see the crater now on the main monitor screen of each tank and could hear the rad warning beeping, and tore through the hot terrain, shooting by the towering crater at top speed. They had to endure two hundred and fifty rads, then three hundred, as they came even with the tower of burning death. Then they were past it, and quickly the built-in Geigers on the outer surface of the Bradleys began signaling a drop. Within ten minutes it had dropped to half, edging below a hundred.

"Didn't feel a thing," Bo said, standing behind Stone, one big hand leaning down on the plastic headrest of the co-driver's seat next to Stone's, his farmboy face grinning.

"You wouldn't feel a thing, but believe me, they went through us. A few hundred more rads and you'd feel it," Stone said coolly as he checked the 360 video scan, noticing a sudden darkening to the west. "Your skin turns red at that high a dosage," Stone went on. "Red like a lobster, it peels off your body like wet tissue paper. Your hair comes out in handfuls if you even touch it, your teeth, fingernails, ooze around as if embedded in putty. You just sort of—fall apart." Stone said it as if telling a ghost story, ending in a ghastly whisper. And it worked. Bo and Simpson both shivered and crossed themselves. Even Excaliber seemed to let out a little groan of depression as he turned over on his private shelf and buried his face into the warm metal away from Stone.

But the darkness on the western horizon continued to hold Stone's attention, and he stopped talking as he looked into the long-range monitor. It was as if the sky were turning black over there. It was only 3:30, Stone saw, checking the tank's autoclock real-time readout. Anyway, night had never fallen like that, he thought, starting to get a little queasy as he took in the magnitude of the approaching sky. It was dark, with a sickly green color to it, the color of corpses, of vomit. The whole thing seemed to be churning and grinding into itself, like some sort of vortex. Streaks of lightning knifed through it everywhere in ribbons of white and blue fire constantly reaching down with loving electric arms to the earth below. But it was the darkness inside of it that was what really caught Stone's attention. It was black, devoid of color, seeming almost to absorb light, and even through the armor, from miles off, Stone could hear it, like a hum a thousand miles off.

Whatever the fuck it was, he didn't like it. And as various warning lights started flashing here and there on the control panel, the tank apparently didn't like it, either. "High pressure disturbance approaching. Wind velocity up to 200 m.p.h. Armor of Bradley III is not sufficient to withstand such pressure."

"Great," Stone spat back. "You goddamned computers always tell me what's wrong, but you don't give me a clue as to how to do something about it." He felt like smashing the goddamned board, as he had done once to his Amiga PC in the bunker. Smashed it to pieces—and then had to spend three months building it again with spare parts from his father's workshop. Putting the top video on quickscan, he searched around the area for the slightest place they might hide. The whole landscape looked about as flat as a blade of glass except for a single rise about a mile in the direction from which the thing was coming. He couldn't believe he was about to order the men *into* the approaching storm, but he knew there was no other way. They had to get protection —and fast.

"We're heading toward that hill or whatever it is, at 237 degrees on your compass. We've got to find cover."

"Heading toward that motherfucking tornado out there," Bull shouted back over the headset, almost blasting out Stone's ears. "You've got to be crazy."

"I'm telling you," Stone said icily, mustering all the authority of command that he had lying around inside his exhausted body, "we've got no choice. The tanks aren't equipped to handle winds of that speed. We need a windbreak between us and—whatever the hell it is. I'm going!" He turned and wheeled the Bradley around in a spinning frenzy of treads and dust. "You can come with me. Otherwise, if I find your bodies after it passes, I'll try to bury them—if I have time." With that he shut up and just tore toward the protruberance in the plain. He looked back and saw the other two tanks just sort of standing there for a few seconds. Then both of them came roaring after him, accelerating like they were coming out of the starting gate. Stone made right for the thing, but having to look into the face of the approaching mass of black clouds that appeared as big as the Rocky mountains was something he found hard to do. The dark curtains of destruction were too powerful. It was almost like looking into the eyes of an angry God. Not for mortal man to see.

As they drew closer, the other two Bradleys right on his heels not twenty yards behind, Stone saw that the rise was not that big at all—not as big as he had hoped. It was a series of five boulders lying side by side, covered with partial coatings of sand. They rose up about eight feet and from end to end were perhaps twenty long. Not enough to give them all cover. The storm loomed right in front of them now, the entire sky and horizon as far as they could see just a writhing pit of utter blackness. And the roar, even through the armoring was growing louder, like an approaching subway that suddenly roars in at one's feet. The tanks were already shaking, buffeted by the advance winds. The men started panicking, looking at one another with clammy, desperate faces.

"Now listen to me," Stone said over the mike. "We've still got a chance. Wedge the tanks together in a *V* facing the boulders. When I say go, we all move forward until we meet. Now!" The three tanks moved cautiously forward until they banged into each other, grinding at the outer coverings of surface steel, pushing at one another like bulldozers.

"All right, stop, stop!" Stone yelled out when it seemed they were as entangled as they could get without wreaking actual destruction. "Turn off the engines, so if there's contact with debris and a gas line somehow gets severed, the feed line will be retracted."

"But it's dark," a voice said almost hysterically, as all three tanks' electrical systems suddenly went dead.

"Relax," Stone said, "there's an auxiliary lighting system —should go on any—" Suddenly a small amber light came on directly overhead in Stone's tank and, he assumed, in the others. They all sat back and waited to see if they would live or die.

CHAPTER

ELEVEN

THE STORM seemed to attack them like a living thing. A thing set on destruction, on annihilation of everything it made contact with. First came the winds, twisting in funnels of gray and brown, ripping up everything they touched. Vegetation, animals, birds—all were consumed in their path, pulled up by hundreds of the chimneys of wind that touched down everywhere and then pulled up again when they'd eaten their momentary fill.

The tanks rocked back and forth, violently banging into one another as the hurricane-force curtains of air slammed into them. The boulders offered some protection, though even they rocked around in place like eggs boiling off the top of their steamers. Within the windstorm were branches, pieces of ground-up cactus, and the corpses of numerous animals and birds, all wildly spinning around as if inside a washing machine. Inside the tanks the men could feel some of the objects slam against the sides or top, banging them like a giant gong, so their brain cavities reverberated with unpleasant sensations.

But the wind was only the start of it, for after several minutes the sheer darkness that Stone had seen through the scan system came upon them. And it was a darkness without a trace of light, a darkness of almost biblical proportions. A darkness of sand. A storm of pure sand extending for twenty miles came roaring over them. And it deposited its load on them like a dump truck making a delivery.

"What the hell's that?" Bo asked nervously as the first sheets of sand drove into the steel plating. It sounded like a thousand little pings, hardly audible themselves, but put together, like a rising chorus. Within seconds the chorus became a scream, then an avalanche of sound. And suddenly they were being thrown around inside the tanks like rag dolls as the three vehicles bounced up and down and every which way and were attacked by the currents of sand that seemed to come in from every possible angle. Stone prayed the tank was as sealed as it was supposed to be, because he knew that to be exposed to the intensity of particles out there would be instant death. A man would be shred to little tunalike flakes in a second. Still, it's hard just to sit quietly, wanting to live, while death rages all around you.

The storm just seemed to get thicker and meaner until the air was nothing but sand, as if the earth itself had risen up and become airborne. And as the waterfall of particles roared into them at velocities up to 250 miles per hour, they etched themselves onto every square inch of the tanks, polishing them, blasting off their surface coating of "impervious" paint. As the sand came, it piled up against the boulders and the tanks, creating a huge dune that quickly rose ten, then twenty, feet in the air. Though it kept sliding down or flying off at the edges, so much more sand was being added to it that the thing somehow grew. It toppled over onto the tanks so that they were nearly covered with the stuff, and then more sand started collecting on the hollow created between tanks and boulders.

The physics of sand waves dictated that the dune rise and fall, rise and fall, as sand was piled onto it and then washed off. But always it grew a little wider and higher. The men inside the tanks had been terrified when they heard the screeching of the winds, then the sands hitting them. But as it grew quieter around them and, after about an hour, absolutely silent, they all became extremely concerned, having no idea what had happened. With tank systems all down, they couldn't even check. Thus they sat, three men to a tank, plus one dog, waiting and contemplating the end of their existences. The air felt somewhat stale, though they all knew about the self-contained oxygen supply, having used it just days before to ward off fire. But it didn't taste good and hardly filled their need for fresh oxygen. So they lay around the floors of the tanks in the semidarkness, in states of panting half asphyxiation.

After two hours, not having heard a thing from outside, Stone at last made the decision to see just what the hell had happened. He rose and turned on the tank's systems, and everything sprang to life, but as it did, warnings flashed from every panel. Stone tried to read what they were saying, but it wasn't at all clear. It was as if the entire operating system of the Bradley were overloaded, as if every defensive sensor were picking up trouble. Stone checked the video scan and got nothing but a pitch-black screen. Then he tried the sighting periscope, with the same result. They seemed to be nowhere, in the middle of nothing. It didn't make sense. Unless—slowly a thought began entering his head that filled him with real fear—they were buried alive. Tanks and all. Beneath feet, perhaps yards, or more. Beneath tons of sand.

He had not only led them all into a death trap but had provided the coffins as well—and had arranged for burial. How thoughtful. Stone could feel a fury rising inside that he knew he had to control quickly, a rage at himself that he had led these men to their deaths. To slow, agonizing deaths through suffocation during which they would have hours to slowly hack their way out of this life, seeing their faces grow bright red and then purple as they gasped for the precious air that wasn't there, for the tank's oxygen supply was limited to three hours at best. Although he knew in a way that it wasn't his fault, Stone accepted the responsibility that all leaders must accept for the men they lead into battle. If a commander's job is to keep his men alive, then Stone had failed miserably. His own death he could handle. But all of theirs? He sat down in a huff in the corner, for the first time at a complete loss as to what the hell to do. He could feel the eyes of Bo and Simpson on him, even the dog. They knew something was up, and knew that he was as lost as they were.

"What the hell is going on?" a voice blared over the earphones that Stone had slipped back on. Well, he couldn't avoid the subject of just what had happened to them forever —as much as he would have liked to. "I'm going to open this hatch and see just where the—" Bull's voice went on from the other tank.

"No, don't!" Stone screamed suddenly, pulling down the mouthpiece in front of his lips. "We're—we're underground. We've been buried in sand. I—I don't know how deep." He could hardly talk and said the last words in a whisper, even though he knew it was important to keep up a good front. He just didn't have it all together right now, that was all.

"Holy shit," Stone heard Bull say, then Hartstein muttered some choice profanities from the other Bradley.

"Look, I don't know what to say to you. To be honest, I don't even know how to proceed. I—" Stone just kept finding himself stuttering whenever he reached for words. There weren't any words.

"Son of a rotten fucking son of a bitch," Bull spat into the microphone, stinging Stone's ears. The aura of deep depression was palpable right through the walls of the three tanks. Every one of them was feeling the same horror, the same sickening nausea in their very souls, that they were about to be buried alive—one of man's oldest, most primeval fears, along with snakes and things that go bump in the night. It wasn't the preferred route of passage.

"Look," Bo said with a little cough, off to Stone's side. He was always too nervous to talk, thinking himself perhaps the stupidest of the attack force. But since no one else was saying a word, he spoke up, self-consciously. "Why don't we just open the hatch a little and see what happens. We got nothing to lose, right? I mean, it's not like we're going anywhere, as far as I can see." Stone hadn't even known Bo had brains enough to make a joke like that, and he looked at the big, pug-nosed farm boy with mild respect.

"You know, I think you're right," Stone said, jumping up from the control seat. "Nothing to lose isn't the half of it." He went to the ladder and climbed the few rungs so his hands could reach and turn the holding lock of the foot-thick circular covering. The bolt moved, but as he pushed up, he couldn't budge the cover an inch.

"Bo, get your ass up here. Lend me some shoulder against this fucker here, it's stuck." Bo was up the ladder in a flash, and though it was a tight squeeze with both of them wrapped around the ladder, they both heaved up with all their might. Slowly the hatchway opened a little—just an inch or two— and dark, grainy sand came pouring in.

"Oh, my God," Simpson said from below them where he had been watching them. "We're going to die. We're going to fucking die. Like this. I can't believe it." He started sobbing loudly, and Excaliber joined in howling, too, so the whole tank was quickly filled with the merry sounds of the terrified.

"Should I close it, should I close it?" Bo screamed out as sand streamed down over his shoulders and head.

"Yeah, pull," Stone said, and they pulled down hard so

that the hatch closed partially again. Now it couldn't be closed all the way, as sand was already spilling in, nor opened. Like an hourglass, the sand started pouring down and onto the steel floor of the Bradley. Even Stone felt an awful kind of icy terror gripping his heart.

"Let's try to open it again," Stone suddenly yelled out, as he couldn't stand just watching the porous grains fall down on them. "Our only chance is that the top of the tank is only covered by a few feet of the stuff. If we push hard, maybe we can dislodge it." Bo looked at Stone skeptically, but he knew they had to do something fast. There wasn't a hell of a lot of time left. They set themselves and heaved up, and this time the hatchway went up nearly a foot. And as it did so, a wall of the stuff started pouring in, all over their chests and legs. Before he knew what was happening, Stone felt Excaliber suddenly leap up from the tank floor and grab onto the edge of the hatchway where the sand was pouring through. The English bullterrier seemed to take a deep breath, then its second, protective eyelids closed over its eyes and it shot into the dark, shifting sands above like a torpedo.

Stone could hardly believe his eyes but had little choice as the animal started kicking and digging up a storm. The sand flew into his mouth and face and down past his shoulders. Stone gagged for a second but held his end of the hatch. He could feel the pressure of tons of sand trying to press it down from above. Bo caught his glance for just a second, and they both had to grin—even in the very jaws of death—at the digging machine that the pitbull had transformed itself into. Its back legs just churned away, almost in a blur, as its head and front paws disappeared into the sand. It dug and it dug, straight up for the surface, knowing instinctively through the moisture and scent it picked up in its sensitive nose just where the nearest air was. As if it were digging a hole into the ground to bury a bone—only this was one straight up instead of down—Excaliber headed inexorably through the sand.

Suddenly the pitbull's head broke surface, and he shook it to clear the sand from over his eyes. Then the slits opened and the canine looked quickly around to make sure it had really done it. It could feel its master grabbing around its back feet, ready to pull it back in, but instead the canine surged forward, pulling itself up onto the sand that covered the tank, nearly dragging Stone along behind it. Feeling the animal move so freely all of a sudden, Stone had to assume it had made it up, and taking perhaps the biggest leap of faith he had ever made in his life, Stone gave Bo a weird grin, closed his eyes and mouth, and followed the dog, letting the pull of its legs as it guided itself out help suck Stone toward the surface. Halfway up, he lost his footing as Excaliber jumped free. Stone nearly panicked, feeling himself stuck nowhere in the middle of a universe of silence. But then he felt Bo push hard from below, and before he knew it, Stone found his head popping free of the grit and he was looking at desert. The two other tanks, just yards away, were totally covered, as were the boulders that had once stood next to them. There was sand as far as the eye could see, as if they had been transported to the Sahara. Stone wiggled his foot below to signal Bo to follow and then set his elbows up on the sides of the sand walls that were slowly falling down the hole his body had created. Slowly, as if pulling himself out of quicksand, Stone lifted his body up and out onto the ridged waves of sand that blanketed the world.

"Thank God," he muttered, looking up at the sky with a quick glance of gratitude. Far to the east, the storm of total death moved on, blocking out that whole portion of the horizon as if a black wall had been erected. But it was past them. Bo came up next. Then the whimpering Simpson. By then so much sand had fallen into the five-foot path they had to travel to the surface that they could pretty much climb in and out of the tank directly, though the thing was two thirds filled with the grit inside. Stone had them take out some shovels from the supply box. Then it was lots of digging as the three of them first shoveled out the top of Bull's tank, then, joined by that crew, freed the men of Hartstein's tank. They all stood around in a kind of daze, just staring at the sand, which stretched off like an endless black beach all around them. After a few minutes of letting their pounding hearts start heading back to normal, Stone spoke.

"Okay, let's take these shovels—and dig. We got three tanks to uncover." It took them nearly six hours of nonstop digging to be able to get all three war machines completely free of their sand tombs. Then another two hours to clean them up, as they had all become inundated with sand. But fortunately the makers of the Bradley III foresaw just about everything, and the armored vehicles came equipped with wet/dry power vacs on the insides, which sucked the sand up and poured the stuff back out into the world from whence it came. As shaken up as the men were, they were all in a good mood. There's something about walking away from the Grim Reaper that puts a twinkle in a man's eye.

CHAPTER

TWELVE

T HEY WOULD never get all the sand out of these tanks—no one would. But the things seemed to be basically functional, and soon they were moving across the recently created desert. They traveled over a good thirty miles of the loose-packed black dirt, the tanks spitting out trails of soot behind them, which rose like the waste of a chemical plant. At last the deposits of the sandstorm came to an end, and they were once again on the hard-packed prairie surface. It felt good just to see living things, even scraggly, flea-bitten cacti, after the sterile lifelessness of the sand world behind them.

As triple peaks lined up along the horizon, Stone brought up the mag grid for this part of the territory and searched for Livermore.

"Distance from present location to Livermore," Stone keyed into the control panel.

"17.587 miles," the computer read out on its display monitor. It flashed the correct compass heading on another panel, and Stone slightly reset the course they had been following, off by less than a degree. The flat land ended, and they came to low foothills that rose up and down like jagged breasts. Rising to the top of the first hill, Stone suddenly was alerted to a radio transmission on the same frequency as the tank's by a panel readout. He had the receiver zero in and through the earphones heard men shouting orders to each other.

"This is K Captain, reporting to L base. We are in pursuit of intruder in Sector-Seven. My force consists of three Bradleys, two Hercules light tanks, two armored vehicles. Intruders are three late-model cars—there should be no need for additional force."

"Copy, K Captain. This is L base." Stone heard the counter signal sweep back through a little bit of static. "Carry on attack but report back every hour—and advise if additional armor or chopper assistance is needed. Out."

It was Patton's boys. Without question. No one else had that military mode of operation. Stone slowed the tanks down until they were moving at only about ten miles per hour. They went down a long, flat slope and then up another that followed some sort of trampled-down migration trail and was just wide enough for a single tank to fit by at a time. At the top of the next slope Stone could see ahead for miles as the land once again dropped off dramatically and formed a five-mile-square plain before rising into high mountains at the far side. And below, Stone suddenly saw through the video monitor, were tanks, rows of them, over two dozen standing side by side. He slammed the brakes on, screamed into the mike for the others to stop, and started backing up before the other two had a chance to throw their big war wagons into reverse, so that Stone was half pushing them back down the hill.

But he didn't want to be seen. If the bastards were really so unprotected—all their heavy armor just waiting there like sitting ducks—Stone and his men might have a chance. He pulled the Bradley off to the side and through a passage in some woods until they were several hundred feet inside, snapping off branches everywhere around them. He came to a clearing just big enough for the three tanks and swung the big machine around as the others followed suit.

"I'm going to check it out on foot," Stone said. "It could be a trap. Keep the systems shut down. And don't broadcast between tanks—they may be tracking us already." With that he climbed the ladder and stepped out the hatchway. As he hit the ground Stone heard a sound right behind him—Excaliber. The pitbull felt like taking a little constitutional. They moved through the woods, and then, rather than going along the open pathway, Stone edged his way up a series of boulder falls until he reached a peak of solid granite, the highest point for miles.

Below he could see it all—the tanks laid out, the jeeps, cannons pointing outward from within a barbed-wire barricade, the same prefab aluminum huts that Fort Bradley had been built with. Stone scanned the base with his field glasses, and then he saw it—the missile silo. Unmistakable, even from a distance. The cone-shaped head that rose six feet out of the earth, the protective shielding over the missile that lay beneath. Stone could hardly believe his luck. The place didn't even seem that well guarded, other than the usual machine-gun posts at all four corners and a jeep that periodically drove around the perimeter, checking the vegetation to make sure that no one was trying to sneak in.

He watched the camp for about two hours, getting all the locations of its sections clear in his mind. Then he searched the surrounding slopes and hills for a possible attack site. There—about two miles off—a flat plateau several hundred feet above ground level. It would give them a perfect trajectory of fire from about three-quarter-mile range. Perfect. Stone set the location of the plateau in his mind, then squirmed back through the thick bushes he had crawled through. He wouldn't wait—there was no need. The sun was just starting to fall, the twilight would be upon them, the night cries of the birds would drown out some óf the sound of the tanks. Yes, they would move—and fast. And then when darkness came, they would open up with prearranged firing angles. The New American Army officers wouldn't even know what was hitting them or from where. He prayed that Patton was down there as well. And that the Fascist madman would die in the hail of fire that was about to descend on them. For he was the problem. With him gone, the whole rotten utopia of mindless, robot citizens would fall apart—just another bad dream from some sadistic little man who would be king.

Stone crawled back through the woods to his tanks and saw that they had posted guards, two men, up in trees with rifles in hand for sniping. Good—they were actually getting it together on their own. He felt a sudden surge of pride in them. The men had been tossed from one terrible situation to another. They had almost been killed three times in the last two days—and still they seemed ready to go on, almost curious about their own skills and abilities to fight, to take on the enemy.

"We're moving out," Stone said as he climbed back into the tank and threw himself down in the metal seat. "We're going for it, man. Right now."

"Don't you think maybe we should—um—talk about this a little, Mr. Stone, sir?" Bo said stumblingly. He was hungry, wanted at least one more good meal before he died.

"No, it's time. Just like when a baby drops, or a shit plops, it's time to strike. I feel it. We're going to do this, we're going to pull it off." Stone's enthusiasm seemed to fire up the others, and they set to preparing for the attack. Even Excaliber, instead of heading toward his usual heated shelf, sensed that something was up and came up alongside Stone, sitting on back legs and watching the same monitor that Stone looked at as he drove the Bradley back out of the woods. Though it was quickly growing darker, Stone clicked on the infrared sighting system and instantly saw the whole world in shifting, wavering, almost three-dimensional images of blues and reds and greens. The enhanced night vision enabled him to see every object ahead of him, and Stone, telling the others to use the night guidance as well, led them slowly across the slope that was around the other side of the low mountain that sheltered the base. They reached the spot that Stone had anchored in his mind, though approaching it from the outside, a dip in the peak of the mountain. It was hard climbing, a lot harder than he had anticipated, with the angle of ascent rising to forty-five degrees. And the surface was not completely firm here and there, so that the treads of the tanks spun fast, kicking out dust and mud. But slowly they made their way up about three hundred feet of such surface until they reached a denser surface.

Here the Bradleys found traction and propelled themselves over the top of the rise and down about a hundred feet of a slope that was not nearly as steep, until they reached the plateau Stone had sighted.

He pulled them to a stop so that they were side by side, and they looked down on the myriad twinkling lights coming from barracks and huts, from floodlights and car lights, cigarette butts, all the signs of human habitation. Stone sighted up his cannon, lowering it with a grinding whine as he set in conjunction the three red laser-generated lines of his sighting system right over the missile silo. With the infrared enhancement he could see clearly through the cloudy, dark night. The sleek metal cone that covered the head of so much death. The other cannons lowered as well, and Stone heard each of the men speak over the mike, softly, nervously.

"Ready here," Bull whispered.

"Here too," Hartstein, said, burping afterward, which made them all chuckle for a split second. "Well, let's kick—" Stone started to say, but an explosion seemed to go off right in front of him, and the entire tank jumped backward. Stone crashed against the back of the seat and felt as if he had whiplash as his head snapped around and around on it like one of those dolls with spring spines. His vision cleared and he saw another explosion, then another, strike ahead of him and then off to the left. The 360 video scan showed tanks, rows of them, on other plateaus all around the one Stone and his men were on. Tanks, covered with camouflage netting, anchored in place. There must have been twenty or more, hopelessly outnumbering Stone's absurdly small attack force. He had been betrayed. They all had. The general had known about it from the start. The whole fucking thing had been a trap. A trick. He had been suckered into the thing like the dumbest idiot who had ever taken a chance at three-card monte, had ever been sure he could guess which almond shell contained the pea, had ever been positive he could pick the ace from the stack of cards held out.

Stone started to drive the tank forward again as he lowered the big 120-mm down into position. If he could just take out the goddamned missile, he could die a little happier, he thought bitterly to himself. Just make it worth it, that's all. Then it was sighted up—or as good as he was going to get things tonight. Through the telescopic sighting lens it looked as if he were right on top of the thing, could almost reach out and touch it. His hand reached for the firing button as another tank volley landed in the dirt just outside the tank, and the Bradley shook violently from side to side. But as he set his finger down to fire the 120-mm, Stone felt something strike the back of his head. He seemed to half slide into darkness, and as he pulled himself out, he took another blow. As Stone sank into a very painful spiral he knew that he had been betrayed, played like a sucker from the start. They'd never had a chance against Patton, not a chance. Then his brain seemed to fizzle like a burned-out light bulb, and he seemed to be swimming in mud, mud that had fists.

CHAPTER

THIRTEEN

WHEN STONE awoke, the first thing he tried to do was lift his hand to touch the ripping pain at the back of his skull. But he couldn't lift his hand—or anything else, for that matter. He was tied hand and foot. Slowly he opened his eyes, which felt like they were stuck together with glue. The light hurt as it entered his pupils, which had seen only darkness for many hours. Brilliant lights all around him, blurry, hard to see. Faces in front of him, walking around him, faces, laughing, but who... He felt confused. Everything was—strange. Stone hardly knew who or where he was. Suddenly, almost at the same instant that his eyes focused on the shapes in front him, his ears seemed to snap on, too, and the world rushed into him with a roar.

"Ah, Stone, so glad to see you're coming around. I was afraid that my man had killed you. He was afraid, you see —afraid that if you didn't go out, you'd kill him. Which is doubtless true." Stone could see the face, the craggy features, the silver hair, but his mind was still half on the blink, and it took him several seconds to realize who was addressing him. When he did, he would just as soon have fallen back into the black ocean he had just been swimming around in.

"General—Pat-Patton," he said, stuttering, slightly amazed that his lips could move, that he could hear his own thoughts. Whoever did it must have hit him real hard. Stone could feel a huge bump the size of a lemon on the back of his head—and dried blood. Still, he could feel his mind clearing as he made a quick scan of his surroundings. He was in an aluminum hut, the curved roof above him. There was a crude wooden floor, sheets of rough plywood placed down on the dirt. The general and five or six men stood around him, wearing the gold emblems of the Elite Corps. And standing with them was Simpson.

"Son of a bitch," Stone groaned out before he even realized he had talked. He had thought it was Bull all along. Had been positive. And he had been wrong.

"Yes, Simpson," Patton said with a thin grin, standing a few feet from his prisoner. "I had him checking you out from the very start—back in boot camp. I always plant one of my own men in with the new recruits. It's saved me a lot of trouble over the years. I was way ahead of you, Stone— from the beginning." The general was so happy at capturing Stone that he let out with a loud, explosive laugh.

"Ah, you bastard, you traitor," Patton said, moving closer, his hands behind his back. "I trusted you above all men—gave you the chance to be next to me, to rule, to—"

"I don't want to rule, asshole," Stone managed to mutter through lips that felt puffy and were not quite working right. "You're a genius, Patton—you could have done a lot for this fucked-up country. But you blew it. And I'd kill you this second if I could."

"Brave words from a man who can't move a muscle." Patton laughed again, turning to the others who had joined in. They were all having a grand old time tonight. Stone looked down for the first time and saw what he was tied to. He was standing, raised up on an X-shaped wooden structure, hands and feet stretched apart and chained to the four ends of the archaic device. His weapons, his knife—everything stripped from him. Reaching inside him for a sudden burst of strength, Stone pulled hard at his wrists, trying to rip free. But the chains only bit into the outer layers of skin leaving red welts, and snapped back after only about half an inch of give.

"Yes, they're quite strong," Patton said, reaching out and tapping the wood on the side, just below Stone's outstretched arm. "We found this, you know—one of the many things my men have dragged in for me. Came from a museum. It was once—believe it or not—used for precisely the purpose we're going to put it tonight." He looked at Stone expectantly. And sure enough, the imprisoned man had to bite.

"And what purpose is that?" Stone asked, giving the general a smirk as if he were his straight man.

"Oh, torture, obviously," the general replied, sweeping his hands around the aluminum-framed hut, which was about fifty feet long and twenty wide. "In fact, to show you how much trouble I've taken to make sure you're 'comfortable' here, I had this place constructed just for you. Because I knew we'd meet again. And that was all I wanted, Stone —to meet you again. I couldn't even go on with my plans until you and I had settled things. And now we will . . . settle things."

He reached forward suddenly, ripping his right hand up from behind his back, and a riding crop struck Stone in the side of the face, leaving a red mark. Stone let his head go with the blow, absorbing most of the force, and then turned back and stared right into the general's eyes.

"I can understand you would want to kill me. And I won't even try to argue you out of it, because I know your mind is made up. But I can hardly believe a man of your stature, your military prowess, would resort to torture. As one fighting man to another, I request that you just shoot me and get it over with."

"Shoot you and get it over with." Patton chuckled, sweeping his hand through his slicked-back silver hair, and again looked around at the others, who immediately followed suit, pealing away as if it were just about the funniest thing they had heard since Caine killed Abel. "No, Mr. Stone, you and I shall get to know each other well tonight—perhaps over the few days, if you live that long, and I sincerely hope you do. You see, I am a believer in the old ways—the warrior ways. The ways of blood and retribution. What you did must be punished, not just because I was wounded, for really it did not anger me. You are just a peon beneath me, a flea, a nothing. But for the sake of the New American Army, for the sake of discipline and law and order, you must be . . . hurt."

"Sounds great," Stone said with a grunt, wishing more than anything that he could scratch an itch at the end of his nose. But instead of a scratch, he got a fist from the general that nearly took his jaw off. Stone's head slammed back against the wood behind him, and he swore he heard something crack—whether it was the wood or his skull, he wasn't sure. Then his eyes cleared again as if out of a kaleidoscopic haze in which there were three of everything. Stone had only gotten back to two of everything when the fist slammed in again and he had to start all over again. The general spent about five minutes on Stone, picking choice punches with a closed right fist with a West Point ring on it, big and brass—to his cheeks and his mouth, his ears and his ribs. The others looked on, cracking their knuckles, letting out little animal grunts of excitement at the blood and the pain.

At last, as Stone hung limply from the chains, Patton stepped back and put one palm under his chin as if trying to judge the scene before him, like an artist checking to see what spot he had missed, what section needed more red.

Stone slowly raised his head up, spat out a large gob of blood, and stared straight into Patton's face. "Is that it? I've had old women with AIDS hit at me harder than that."

"Oh, no, Mr. Stone, that isn't it at all. That was just the first course, the appetizer. My men here would like a few words with you as well." Stone looked into each face as the men came toward him. He wanted to remember them, wanted to memorize every feature of the bastards, because if somehow, some way, he lived, he would track them down to the ends of the fucking earth. The first fist hit him under the ear, snapping his head to the left, but halfway in recoil, the opposite ear took another shot, and like a volleyball, he bounced back and forth. Then he felt boots slamming into his stomach, his back. He wanted to fall down, to cover himself, try to protect himself from the blows. But chained up, he was helpless, couldn't move a muscle, a finger. And that was the most horrible thing of all.

Stone didn't know how long the blows rained down on him. He couldn't pass out, though he prayed to. But he was too fucking tough. He felt them all, felt his body and flesh and brains being slammed around like liver in a Cuisinart. For some reason, in the middle of it all, he suddenly thought of Excaliber and wondered how the dog was. And hoped that it would do okay without him. Damned dog—he wished he'd had time to say good-bye. But then you never knew when you were about to die. At last, after what must have been twenty minutes or half an hour, they stopped and fell back panting, their fists bloody, knuckles broken on many of their hands. Hands that had hurt themselves on the flesh of Martin Stone.

And still, as they looked at each other, grinning, feeling real good about the damage they'd done, about being such macho men, Stone somehow opened one eye and looked at them. Lips that were bloodied and torn, spat out a whole little river of blood, and the mouth hoarsely whispered, "Is that it? I've gotten worse from midgets with one arm." Stone tried to smile but it hurt too much, and his head sank back the few inches it had risen. But the eye, the single eye that was still open—the other was swollen to the size of a lime and closed shut—just kept looking at them, mocking them. Like the smile of the Cheshire cat, the eye seemed to float there on his face, a blood-coated symbol of the fact that Martin Stone could not be conquered.

CHAPTER

FOURTEEN

THEN IT was more of the in-again out-again consciousness of Stone's brain. He really didn't know where he was or where the hell anything else was, either. But he knew he was Martin Stone. And in his mind he kept saying that over and over to himself. For he was spinning too fast, too hard, to let go. If he did, he might go over a falls from which there was no return. He felt the X-shaped torture device he was on being turned on its back —because he was suddenly looking straight up at the overlit ceiling of the hut. There was more laughter, gales of it, and then his clothes were being cut or ripped right off his body, and something was smeared all over him, something sticky and coating. Even in his semi-comatose state it didn't feel pleasant, stinging sharply where it touched against broken skin and blood-oozing wounds. Stone wanted nothing more than to reach down and clean the sticky skin, but as he did so, his hand again snapped against the chain that confined it, and with a sigh of resignation Stone steeled himself to his imminent death. He just wished he didn't have to go so coated with slime.

Then he was being carried. He knew because he could feel his stomach going up and down and he felt like he was going to puke. And the next thing he knew, he did—to his side—which shot down onto one of those carrying him, who smashed into Stone's back with something hard. The pain sent him back to the periphery of total darkness. He didn't know how long it had been, then one eye opened and he saw the sky above, stars leering down like a drunken crowd, cheering on his annihilation. Then he was being lowered and he could feel the cold dirt of the prairie floor below his back. And when he opened his one working eye just a crack the size of a razor blade, he could see them again, standing above him like ogres a hundred miles high, and their faces were all contorted, their lips wide and flapping. And for some reason he couldn't hear again, but he knew what they were doing. Knew that they were laughing, laughing at him.

Stone suddenly felt terribly cold and, realizing he was out in the middle of the Northern Colorado desert, naked, with some sticky icing all over him, wondered, just for a second or two, what the hell they were doing. Then, as the cold stiffened up his muscles so that the bruises and welts and broken blood vessels from the hundreds of kicks and punches that had been rained down upon him suddenly hurt as if he were on fire, Stone mercifully, as if his body had just become supersaturated with pain and couldn't take another drop, lapsed into the comforting darkness once again.

When he came to next time, it was quick. All of a sudden his eyes opened and his mind was much clearer than it had been. They were gone, at least as far as Stone could see, though he could only turn his head from side to side. He was in the middle of nowhere, with cacti rising in the moon and starlit darkness. There were large mounds every thirty feet or so, towering columns of packed dirt. Most of them were half collapsed, their walls broken in various places like a chimney from a long closed factory.

Jesus, he was thirsty. His mouth felt like he had been chewing marbles, broken marbles. His lips felt huge, like pillows, and he could feel blood still dripping slowly from all over him. Stone wondered how he looked, narcissism raising its eternal head even in the midst of all this. He wondered if they'd fucked him so bad that his face was all misshapen, his teeth gone—if he was hideous now, like so many of the poor wounded and radiation-burned bastards he'd seen already in his travels. But it was hard to tell what had been particularly damaged because everything was in pain, every square inch of his flesh and bones felt like they had been put through a shredding machine. He managed to crane his neck just enough to look down at the rest of his body. He was as naked as the day he was born but covered with some syrupy stuff. In spite of it all, Stone let out a laugh, which hurt like hell. He looked like the fucking tar baby from Uncle Remus. Well, at least the bastards who wanted to do him in were imaginative. Stone had to give Patton and his sick crew that. But exactly what they had in mind for him escaped him. To have the syrup harden in the frigid night air? Turn him into some kind of corpse candy bar enclosed within a frozen sugary coating?

To his displeasure Stone was becoming more conscious by the second. He much preferred the other place. But his mind cleared as the cold set in and his one working eye opened more than just a slit so he could pretty much see the whole fucking world around him. And he didn't like what he saw. Ants. Just a few to the left of his head where he had turned, but farther off, coming out of one of the high mud towers, were more of them—a lot more. By the light of the silvery moon Stone could see ugly little faces drawing closer to him. The advance scouts. One approached straight toward him—it was a big son of a bitch for an ant, a good inch long with mandibles big enough to not want it to get too close. It made a beeline for Stone's nose, as if the finishing line of its race. And as Stone looked on, the reddish-black insect suddenly leapt forward and landed on the tip of his bloody nose. Without even an introduction it opened the half-inch-wide jagged jaws and slammed them closed on a little piece of hanging flesh.

Stone couldn't believe the sound his scream made as it left his lips. He flung his head back and forth, dislodging the little bastard, which flew off with a tiny chunk of Martin Stone for its reward. Stone's scream stopped after a few seconds, but his heart started beating so fast that he could hardly breathe through his snot- and blood-choked throat. He had screamed not so much from the pain, though it hurt like a razor being sliced slowly across his nerves, but because he suddenly realized what the madman Patton had in store for him. To be attacked by these things. By these thousands of little mouths. Mouths that could, from just the one bite that Stone had received so far, be incredibly painful.

"Shit," he growled up into the night air. "Shit," he spat out at the stars staring amusedly down, at the three-quarter moon, looking like a punctured ball about to fall from the sky. "I don't want to go like this, you son of a bitches." Stone didn't know if he was addressing the general or the galaxies, but it hardly mattered. Neither were listening.

Suddenly Stone just let his whole body go limp. He lay there absolutely motionless, as the crickets and the wind joined together in a whistling, crackling chant of the darkest part of night. Chant of death, of teeth on flesh, of jaws cracking open skulls. Well, at least the bastard wouldn't shoot off the A-bomb he had threatened to. He had Stone now, there was no reason any longer. Not that it was going to help America, Stone knew. The man would probably be able to carry out his dark plans of absolute control and controlled extermination. Stone was just as glad he wouldn't be around to see it. Yeah, all things considered, it was probably just about time to kick off. He tried to rationalize in his mind, tried to get into the idea of death, groove on it.

But he didn't groove on it when the second scout ant leapt up onto his cheek and took out a lobster-claw-sized chunk of prime human. Stone involuntarily yelled out again. He just hated how it felt when those snapping turtle–like jaws bit into him. But he didn't have time to dwell too much on that one, for another burning sensation ripped into his ear. Then his neck. Then his foot and leg. And though Stone did his best to roll and twist, the best he could manage was a few inches one way or another. But only a few of the miniature monsters were dislodged. The rest took as much as they could carry of the dripping flesh and popped back down onto the prairie floor, heading immediately back to the colony tower some thirty feet off. And as they went, they passed hordes of the advancing columns of main army ants. These had even larger mandibles, jaws, and bodies for carrying huge loads of supplies back to the colony. And even as Stone struggled and shouted curses in mortal horror, the ants leapt up from the ground by the dozens, then the hundreds. And they were everywhere on him, and Martin Stone could feel himself being slowly eaten up, could feel the outer layers of his flesh already being torn off. And he knew with growing horror that it would take a long time for him to die. Perhaps many hours. And he would feel and know and sense every second of what was already sending him to the brink of absolute madness: the death of ten million bites.

CHAPTER

FIFTEEN

MARTIN STONE entered a world of pain that few men get to experience. Many have died perhaps as painfully—by fire or acid—but these, at worst, kill within minutes. Stone would not be so lucky. He kept thinking that it wouldn't get worse, but it did, as more and more of the writhing bodies swept over him, covered him in a blanket of their consuming passion. But as men adjust to even the most terrible of situations and just try to keep things from getting worse, Stone tried to keep the rippling little brown bodies from his eyes. That was going to be the most horrible. Seeing them as they actually ate right into the socket. Stone wondered what he had done to offend whoever was up there minding the store.

Suddenly he was doused with cold liquid, and a shudder ran down his body. He opened his eyes to see a woman, clad in deerskin and bear hide, holding a large gourd filled with water, which she dumped on him again. Stone sputtered as some of it rushed into his mouth, but the terrible pain was lessened all over him as the water washed the army of flesh-takers away. As the woman bent over him to one side, Stone could see that she was an Indian, with long black hair pulled back inside her fur collar and coppery, smooth skin. And even in the midst of the most wrenching pain Stone had ever experienced, he could see that she was beautiful. She bent out of view, and Stone could feel some cutting or pulling against the chains that held him. His right hand snapped free, and he pulled it down, flexing it and stretching it. The muscles felt like they had turned to rock, the veins and nerves frozen like wet ropes in the Arctic.

Then she was around the other side, and his left hand came free. Then his legs, too, were released from the torture rack, and she reached down, helping Stone rise to his feet. He could barely stand, and she supported him as he felt his legs turn to rubber bands and waver wildly beneath him. Everything was spinning, and he could see from the look in her eyes that he looked bad, real bad. She scanned him up and down, and Stone remembered that he was naked and a sense of modesty came over him that made him so dizzy, he tumbled back to the dirt. She pulled him by the shoulders several yards away from the still streaming lines of ants, searching for their missing meal, angry and moving fast. She helped Stone into some deerskin pants and shirt and fitted moccasins on his feet. Just being away from the fuck-ing mandibles and protected from the subfreezing tempera-ture made Stone feel like he was at Club Med basking in the sun. Almost.

As he lay half propped up against a stump of an ancient petrified tree, Stone saw the woman drag a body out of the shadows and bring it up to the X. It was an NAA'er, his throat slit, Stone could see through blurred eyes. The woman attached the body's hands and legs to the chains, not that he was going anywhere, and then stepped back. Already the ants started closing in, not even aware that they had been given a substitute meal. But then it hardly mattered to them. All human beings tasted pretty much the same.

"Come on," the Indian woman said as she came back to Stone and helped him to his feet again.

"Who—who are you?" he asked, wondering if all his teeth were still there, as his mouth felt real strange, as if he had chewed a whole stick of cotton candy at once and there was little room to breathe or talk.

"I'm Meyra, daughter of Fighting Bear, of the Cheyenne. Come, we must go. Go fast. I killed two of their guards— they'll check on you at dawn. I know them."

"You killed them? You know—" Stone asked, both confused and just wanting to ask her something so he could look into those brown eyes, which drew him in like oases of perfect calm and beauty in the midst of his terrible, mind-blasting pain.

"Shut up, mister," the woman said, and Stone could feel as she held him with one arm around her shoulder, the other pulling him up by a grip on the outside of the deerskin he was wearing, that she was strong, very strong. But still he felt himself starting to give out after just a few steps. His body just didn't want to work, things were broken, gears fallen out of alignment here and there.

"You've got to help me a little," she said, her face just inches from his so he had a sudden insane impulse to kiss her, which he didn't. Even delirium wouldn't be explanation enough. "I can't carry you completely on my own. Try, just try, to keep pumping your legs—I'll guide you." She pulled him closer against her so he was half covered by one side of her thick fur coat.

"Trying," Stone said with a thin smile. "Tryin', I swear I am." And again everything was just sort of surreal, as it had been for quite a while now. Alice in Wonderland had nothing on Martin Stone. His eyes kept opening and closing like doors for the birds on cuckoo clocks. Somehow he kept just sending the command to his legs to move, and they did—up to a point. Every few steps a knee would give out, or a thigh just felt like it wasn't there. But she would catch him as he started to go, and that would wake him enough to help her out. But it was rough going, every step of it.

Suddenly she threw him down onto the ground, diving down alongside him, and Stone, after catching his breath from the blow, started to ask her what the hell was going on. But she slammed a hand over his mouth. Lights appeared about fifty yards dead ahead of them, and they heard the sound of a motor. It was one of the NAA jeeps out on perimeter patrol. But they hadn't been alerted yet about Stone's escape and went by with twin beams piercing the night, without even noticing the two figures lying facedown behind a thick cactus.

When they were completely out of view, Meyra rose again and pulled Stone to his feet.

"Sorry," she said with just a glimmer of a smile flickering across her face. "I had to shut you up."

"You can shut me up anytime you want," Stone whispered back, his throat hardly capable of speech now, as the cold completely swelled up the damaged cells that had been broken by the beatings. She dragged him on for what seemed like miles, Stone feeling more dead than alive but aiding her with every bit of remaining willpower he had. He knew that if he faltered or fell, he was a dead man. And he didn't relish another meeting with his ant buddies back there, nor to see her graceful face eaten away until it was blood-splattered bone. And those thoughts gave him the energy to go on. Stark terror is a strong motivator.

At last she stopped, and he felt himself leaning on something, something quite pungent. He opened his eyes and saw a horse—more likely a mule, as its shoulders were lower than his.

"Get on," she said, still whispering, as if she were afraid they'd be heard out there in the middle of nowhere. He leaned toward the skinny thing and tried to climb on but just couldn't muster the strength in his legs or arms for the job. He felt embarrassed, stupid. A man always wants to be strong, particularly in front of a woman he finds attractive. And Stone could hardly move a muscle. A three-year-old child would have beaten him at arm wrestling at that moment.

"Come on, big boy," she said with a trace of amusement in her voice. "Let's try to get this load on. After that you can rest." She grabbed him around the ass, taking a good handful with each hand, and started hoisting him up on the thing.

"Goddamn fucking son of a bitch, mother—" Stone snorted under his breath like a madman, so furious was he at his super-weakened state. But as she pushed and he grabbed hold for all he was worth with his half working arms, fingers gripped around the mule's scraggly mane, somehow he made it up and onto the creature's narrow back. Stone was draped right over the thing, its pointed backbone poking into his stomach, which didn't need any more work done on it right now. She took the reins and led the animal forward, and the rocking, up-and-down motion instantly made Stone feel like his guts were on fire. But he knew he couldn't even raise himself up. Hardly able to breathe, his face turning red, he lay draped like a blanket, his face staring straight down at the cold, brown dirt passing by below him.

Stone had totally lost track of time, so he had no idea how long they bounced along like this. It felt like centuries, but it just as easily could have been hours or even minutes. But at last they came to a complete stop, and Stone felt several pairs of hands peeling him off the back of the exhausted pack mule. Then he was being carried hand and foot into some sort of tepeelike structure and laid down on a soft bed made of furs, warm and comforting like a woman's arms. Stone felt his stomach relaxing, ever so slightly, for the first time in hours. The others disappeared from the conical-shaped buffalo-hide structure, and she closed the flap behind so they were totally sealed in. She struck something in the center of the floor of the tepee, which was a good twenty feet wide at its base, tapering to about two at the top, which was opened up for the release of fumes and smoke. A fire burst into being, and the warm flames instantly fell against Stone's face some eight feet away.

"Now, let's see what the bastards did to you," she said, coming over to him and standing beside the bed. As if he were a sick and limp child, she took off first the long coat, then the deerskin pants and moccasins she had clothed him in on the desert. He vaguely knew what was going on, as a deep grayness had now descended on him. The heat of the fire relaxed him more and more. And he could feel her hands moving over him, up and down. She seemed to be washing him with something, then drying it off. Then putting an ointment over him that instantly felt soothing and cool. In a way Stone felt embarrassed being naked while she worked all over him. But then he had always been proud of his strong swimmer's body and his well-endowed other features. Still, he didn't know what he looked like anymore, after the beatings and the ant picnic on his chest and face. And for some reason, in the midst of all the madness and death around him, Stone found the most important thing was that he wouldn't be hideously ugly—like the monsters he had seen out there.

Then he did at last fall into the darkness again. But this time it was a loving darkness. A darkness in which the hands continued to run across him and the warm fires caressed him, and the furs beneath his back felt so warm and endlessly soft, as if he could swim in them. And Stone wondered in his dreamy state if perhaps he'd died and this was heaven.

But as he did fall into a deeper, almost comalike sleep, the heaven turned to hell, as the ants were upon him again. Only this time he was both in his body feeling it all and ten feet above it, floating there like some kind of bird, as he watched himself slowly disappear beneath the churning jaws of the carpet of blood-soaked ants. He could see his outer layers of skin disappear, then the muscles beneath. Then his raw, pumping arteries and organs were attacked and eaten by the things one tiny bloody bite at a time. Until he was just a single beating heart lying on the prairie floor surrounded by ivory bones that glowed in the moon-carved night. And then the ants closed in on the heart as it seemed to almost roll away from them, propelled on little arterial feet. But they caught it, and they bit into that too. And when the last bite had been taken, there was nothing left. And Martin Stone floated in his dream above the nothing that was now himself. And he felt himself crying that he was dead—more that this body was gone and he wouldn't have a burial, wouldn't even sink into the dirt and become flowers and trees. And the tears fell and watered the ground where his body had been, wetting the bones with little waterfalls of liquid silver that danced across them.

Suddenly he was awake again. She was sitting next to him and stroking his face slowly, with such delicacy and grace that it sent goose bumps up his spine, an electric sense of her presence and warmth.

"You were crying in your sleep," she said softly.

"I—I—" Stone started to protest, not even knowing what it was he was protesting.

"Shh," she said, again laying her fingers across his lips. "Don't protest. All men—especially the men of my tribe—are afraid to cry. But it releases the poisons, the toxins. It is the body's way of healing from the inside, as I try to heal you from the outside." She pulled back the blanket that had been half covering him and reached down for a gourd filled with a green paste.

"It is just as well you awoke," she said. "It is time for me to put another layer of medicine on you."

"What is it?" Stone asked, his one good eye looking up at her and trying to get her in focus in the flickering rays of the fire that burned calmly in the center of the tepee. His mind felt a lot clearer than it had before—at least he could remember his name, knew vaguely where he was, and probably could have added up two and two, which was a hell of a lot more than he could have accomplished just hours before.

"I wonder if you really want to know," she said, smiling down at him, and he saw that she was even more beautiful than he had thought. She took a handful of the strong but not repulsive-smelling stuff, slapped it down on his chest, and then began smearing it off in all directions as if fingerpainting across him. "It's rattlesnake liver, cactus pulp, lizard tails, bat saliva, and two kinds of poisonous plants, fatal if eaten. Satisfied?"

"I shouldn't have asked." Stone smirked, remembering as he did so that he shouldn't smirk, for an electric jolt of pain shot across his jaws and mouth.

"You have a beautiful body," she said softly as she continued to spread the ointment across him. She looked coyly at him. "Does that embarrass you?"

"It embarrasses me because I keep thinking they really fucked me up—that I look like hamburger. Tell me, do I have all my teeth? Does my right eye work, or is it . . . gone?"

She burst out laughing and slapped him on the chest, which sent waves of pain through his whole chest and stomach. "Sorry," she said, suddenly putting her hand over her mouth as she realized she had hit him. "I laughed because— no, you have not lost anything, as far as I can see. You were beaten up—that I can see—badly. Every part of you is black and blue. And those ants, they just started in on you, but I got there pretty fast, once I saw them lay you out." Stone felt himself growing dizzy again, but he struggled against it. He was getting tired of heading for dreamland whenever he got a little breathless.

"Who—who—are you?" he choked out, suddenly coughing, and she raised his head and fed him some strong herb-flavored water that soothed his throat almost immediately.

"I am—we are—Cheyenne," she said, her face taking on a proud, defiant look. "There are few of us left now—very few. But those who are, are tough—and we survive."

"Why—did—you save me." Stone asked, suddenly able to speak slightly louder as the Cheyenne throat medicine seemed to smooth things out in there a little.

"We—hate Patton," she said bitterly, getting a look on her face that Stone was thankful was not directed against him. "He has killed many of what few of my people are left," she said, her eyes going from calm brown to storms of hate. "We lived not bad lives after the disaster that befell the country. After all, we had little to lose compared to others— to the white man. And as we gave up our reservation life and readapted to the hard land, we got strong again. Those of us who survived. But when Patton showed up a year ago and built his fortress, at first we thought that perhaps the government would be friendly to the Cheyenne even if no one else would. And those who went to meet with him were tortured and killed—every one of them. One was my father, Fighting Bear, a strong and gentle man. Then he hunted us down, sent out unit after unit to get us. Tanks, shooting Indians off horses, cannon blowing up tepees and children. It was like the good old days all over again," she said bitterly. "Like the first massacres when this land was stolen from us."

"I know," Stone said, looking up sympathetically at her. He knew what it was like to lose those closest to you, to say the least. "I guess Indians are on his extermination list too."

"We saw your tanks come into the valley—we see everything that goes on for miles around. And the battle—the trap you were led into. When I saw them bring you out of the fort, I knew you were the leader of the strike force. They would never waste all their time, have General Blood himself come out for the occasion. So I helped you."

"We've got to get out of there," Stone said, suddenly rising up on his elbows, or trying to, as both appendages collapsed instantly beneath him like ropes. "The bastard has an atomic missile. When he finds out I'm gone, he'll—"

"Shh," she said again, pushing him back down with the palm of her hand. "It will wait until morning. Even death has the etiquette of letting a man get a good night's sleep."

CHAPTER

SIXTEEN

MEYRA LIT a stick of strong-smelling herbs that made Stone feel as if he were floating even higher than he already was, and then she spread the Cheyenne healing paste down over his arms and chest and stomach. When she reached his manhood, she didn't pause but spread the green stuff there, too, and Stone, being a man, began to stiffen. He sensed her breath coming more quickly, the heat of her body just inches away from him. She held him in her hands as he grew like a tree in time-lapse photography.

"Oh," she moaned between suddenly clenched teeth, looking down at what she held. And then it was as if she entered another realm of herself, for her back arched like a cat's and she moved alongside him, groping frantically with both hands at Stone's organ. She groaned again, and Stone heard himself make a similar noise as she ran her hands and fingers all around the fleshy staff like it was something mystical, a wand of power from some magic kingdom. She began running her hands from the base to the tip, over and over, making him even bigger and thicker so that he felt his own hips thrusting up in involuntarily animal motions. Suddenly she was bending over him, and her hot lips and mouth enclosed on the enflamed knob. Stone felt himself sink nearly all the way into her, and he could hardly take the sensations. His body still ached in every spot from the experience of the last twenty-four hours, yet her burning fingers and mouth were driving him into a frenzy. And somewhere inside of him, at the deepest part of the sexual motor that drives a man, a wave of desire and lust and the will to live overtook him. And he wanted her, desperately. Wanted the strength to take her as a man should.

He commanded his sore, bruised arms to rise, and somehow, as if he were pulling the strings of a puppet—only the strings were made of rubber and the arms just sort of dangled—Stone made the half dead limbs move. He raised them forward through the air, made the fingers reach for her firm, hanging breasts, which fell over his stomach as she moved up and down on the long, stiff shaft, emitting groans and whistles of animal desire and sexual hunger. He cupped one of the firm, copper-colored breasts in his hands, and the nipple seemed to harden and rise up between his fingers. He squeezed it hard, and she groaned and took him even deeper into her throat, opening up for him, the way a woman does for a man she wants. Then he was just kneading her breasts with both hands, squeezing them back and forth, almost like a child squeezes its mother.

Then he wanted her. He let his hands fall down around her waist, and he pulled her up toward him. Slowly she came at his command, and he lay back down on the bear furs as she was now kneeling on top of him. She rested the palms of her hands on his chest and then sank down on top of him, letting her lips slowly rest against his. She kissed him softly over and over, her hips pushing against his. He could feel the heat coming from between her legs, and in the throes of passion that Stone could hardly believe he was experiencing in his racked and torn body, he reached down and cupped her around the furry slope that was releasing its own perfumes. She groaned again and seemed to buck beneath his grip, then spread her legs wide, giving him access to her. She slid her garments off as he touched her and opened her with his fingers.

Then she was lying atop him again, and she raised herself up and found his manhood with her hand. She placed the swollen tip just inside the flesh petals beneath her reddish fur and then slowly lowered herself on it. Her eyes closed, and her lips parted, as a hiss of air came from between her teeth. Slowly the spear of turgid flesh slid deeper and deeper into the recesses of her body. Stone felt his own urgent writhings as his body and limbs seemed to vibrate. From where he didn't know, but suddenly he felt infused with strength, and he pumped up hard into her to meet her descending flesh.

Suddenly he plunged all the way into her, to the very hilt of himself, and she seemed almost to half faint so that he had to catch her with his hands as her face came down toward him. She was so beautiful by the dancing flames of the fire, her black hair spread down her shoulders and back, her slim, perfect body above him, her femaleness fitted over him like a sheath over a sword. Suddenly he thrust hard up into her, overcome with pure animal lust. She gasped and sank down deeper onto him, opening, opening like the petals of a flower open for the sun. And before he knew it, Stone was driving up into her again and again, his hands gripped firmly around her waist so he held her in check above him, while his hips just pistoned into her, driving his staff to the very depths of her burning core.

Then she seemed to go mad atop him, riding him, bouncing up and down to meet his thrusts. Her mouth opened wider and wider, as if she were a fish gasping for air, and her breasts seemed to swell and grow, the nipples rising, begging to be licked and bitten. Her whole body seemed to glow and pulse with a reddish aura, and he could feel the electric currents between them, the very primal energies of man and woman, mingling with and recharging each other. Then they were both going mad, over the edge, devoid of humanness, but just pure animal spirit desiring nothing more than to crush themselves against the other, take and be taken, push and open, explode and ooze.

Stone could feel himself at the edge, a lava of lust building deep inside himself. And he could feel by her moans and gasps and by the increasing jerking spasms of her body as she seemed like a spineless puppet, writhing around atop him, that she was almost there too. And he pushed even harder, deeper, until he could be no farther into her, her soul, and he held himself there, extended to his full length. She seemed to go mad, flopping atop him like a fish out of water, her whole body snapped and jerked, her head rolled from side to side as she slid down on him, taking every molecule of him. Then she screamed, and her back spasmed up and down its length and she ground down against his stomach, wrapping herself completely around him. Stone pulsed and exploded inside of her in a nova of heat and gasps. He felt the steaming liquid rise in him, and then, like a geyser of steam, he erupted into her, pumping, pulsing like a beast alive within her.

"*Yanna,*" she said minutes later as she lay naked and covered with a sheen of sweat and half the healing paste she had smeared on him, and she looked almost greenish over her coppery skin as the low flames of the fire wriggled back and forth in waves of red and orange. "Yanna," she said again in the softest of whispers, tracing her finger softly up and down his spine as he lay facedown, naked, on a shining black pelt.

"*Yanna?*" he asked in a whisper from out of the love-scented semidarkness.

"Lover," she answered like a dove cooing. "The giver of

love, really, is how you would say it in my language." So he was a *yanna*, a giver of love—and a *nadi*,—giver of death. If he had to choose one, Stone thought as he reached out and traced the perfect curve of her pomegranate breasts, then he would make love, not war.

CHAPTER

SEVENTEEN

W HEN HE awoke the next morning, Stone's eyes were fixed right on the opening at the top of the tepee, so he saw immediately that the day was cold. Silver sky and blank walls of clouds rolled overhead like an endless sheet of metal. He felt as if he were on fire—the temperature in the tepee had risen considerably overnight. He reached for her but she wasn't there, and Stone rose up to look around. As he did he realized that—lo and behold—he could actually move. He didn't feel great, to say the least. Everything hurt like he had received about a million razor cuts and a stomping from a pack of dinosaurs. But as he hadn't even been able to support his body the night before, anything was an improvement.

"I'm here," a voice said, kneeling over the fire. Stone smelled strong odors wafting over toward him with an almost palpable presence. "Just cooking some breakfast." She smiled over at him. "Man like you needs to eat." She wore only a sort of loincloth, hardly more than a strap of leather around her triangle of moist, reddish hair, and a deerskin vest, open down the middle so her breasts stood out, draped on each side by the soft tan hide. Stone felt himself starting to get excited again and could hardly believe it. He should have been dead—yet here he was, ready to fuck his brains out. The women was either the sexiest thing he had ever laid eyes on or she was a witch. There was no other answer.

"Are you a witch?" He grinned as he propped himself up on a bunched-up old bison head that she used for a pillow— clothes hung on its horns, which circled out from both sides around the end of the bear-fur bed. She carried a steaming bowl toward him and kneeled down on the bed so that their legs were just touching.

"Yes, a witch," she answered as she lifted a wooden spoon full of a porridgelike substance. "A witch over men —whose hearts or bodies I crave. A man like you." He started to answer, but as he opened his lips she thrust the spoonful of hot chow into his mouth and he gulped it down hard. It took him a good ten seconds to even sort out the taste—something like oatmeal and chopped liver.

"What the hell is it?" Stone asked as she held a second steaming spoonful up to his lips.

"This time I'll save you your stomach." She laughed. "And I won't tell you—remember what happened last night. All that matters is that it's super-high protein and will help your body recover." She pushed it into his mouth, and as his stomach hadn't rejected the first load, Stone took it down, and damned if it didn't taste pretty good once you got past how it looked and smelled. After he had finished off two bowls of the stuff and nearly half a gallon of some "medicinal" liquid she gave him, Meyra helped him get dressed as she got into her things too.

"The others are waiting for us," she said to him as she stood up on her toes and kissed him quickly on the mouth. "Are you ready to go? There is much to do and little time. Can you walk?"

"Yes," Stone said, pushing her off so he could try to walk around on his own. "I think so." He made a wide circle around the inside of the tepee. He felt light-headed, but nothing like the totally numb, leg-dropping zombie state he had been in.

"It would seem your treatment worked, Doctor," Stone said, going over to her and pulling her close, up against his bearskin coat, cupping her ass through her own thick garb.

"It is passion that keeps a man alive," she said with a faint smile. "All ancient medicines and magic systems are based on that. I just brought out—shall we say—what is already inherent in you."

"I'll say," Stone said, looking deep into those eyes he couldn't get enough of. "Pulled out, and up, and every which way. And I wouldn't mind doing it a—"

"Come on, lover boy," she said, starting toward the exit of the tepee, half pulling him along by the collar. "We're holding up a meeting." Stone walked outside behind her as she shut the bison-skin flap of the Indian structure. His eyes took a few seconds adjusting to the light of the cloud-shrouded day. Both eyes, he was pleased to note, were still working, albeit at half mast. Stone stumbled forward a few steps, until she took him by the elbow and led him down a dirt path past two other tepees. They came to a small fire with two long logs on each side of it. Stone wasn't sure what he had been expecting, but what he saw was definitely not it. The eight or so Cheyenne who sat before him hardly looked the type of Indian that Stone had in his mind of how Indians should look. None of them wore bearskin but denim jackets of all different colors, jeans, and boots. Several of them had earphones on, Walkmans attached to their belts, and seemed to be listening to jazz or rock that Stone could dimly hear floating through the insect cracklings and fire poppings of the early morning.

He sat down on an empty space on one of the logs, and Meyra sat beside him. He looked around at the other faces for jealousy or anger—after all, he had just spent the night with one of their women. But he didn't see it—just a sort of removed curiosity about him. And neither hostility nor friendliness was offered.

"You guys don't look like Indians," Stone said, knowing as he said it that it was the wrong thing to say.

"And you don't stink like a white man," one of the others, several scars gouging along one side of his face, replied. "How the hell are Indians supposed to look?"

"Hey, lighten up," Meyra said, looking around at them. "Guy almost lost his life fighting the general. Put his cock right on the line." Stone was slightly startled by her use of the curse and then realized that he was again judging everything by some notions of an America that was long gone. Women shouldn't curse, Indians shouldn't wear denim and have Walkmans. He tried to banish all the bullshit from his head and just take them as they were.

"So what's the scene?" one of them directly across from Stone asked, his hair slicked back beebop-style, a gold earring in one ear. He had the same copper skin and strong features that Meyra did, and Stone knew instantly that he was her brother. "Are you—the commander of the tank force that was captured? Commander Stone?" he asked.

"That's me." Stone smiled back, feeling friendly toward all of them, considering the night he had just been given as a kind of supreme reward for having been hacked to within an inch of his life. And now that he had been with her, Stone couldn't say he wouldn't go through it all again. "But as for being a 'commander,'" he explained, "If you saw the outcome of my attack, you'd know that's not a word that should be used in front of my name."

"Don't bust your balls—there's always someone ready to do it for you," the Indian, apparently the leader of the group, said, offering a slight smile. "You were set up—we saw them baiting a trap days ago but didn't know who the hell they were baiting until it was too late."

"Tell me—my crew, the tanks, there was a dog . . ." The words spilled out of Stone's mouth in a waterfall of worry.

"One of the tanks was destroyed. The men were taken away. As for a dog, sorry, Stone, I didn't see nothing. But then I was probably two miles off, looking through these cheap-shit binocs." He snapped his fingers against a pair that hung around his neck. "Name's Little Bear—named after my dad." He held out a hand. "Glad to meet you, Stone. I'll be honest with you—I've never been a great fan of the white man. I mean, let's face it, all the great killers were white, and you don't need no Plato to tell you that. But any enemy of General Patton is a friend of mine—especially someone willing to give his skin. We know of his missile too. Though just recently did we learn of his decision to use it. We have a contact on the inside there. A missile tech—a friend of Sis's here." He pointed with his eyes toward Meyra, who looked into the fire with deep concern. Little Bear spat into the flames, and the little droplets sizzled and popped into mid-air.

"He would destroy our entire land, Stone—if he sets that fucking thing off. A land we have inhabited for thousands of years—gone. But we've had no way to stop him—there are just these ten of us. The rest of the tribe is split up over the whole northern part of Colorado and up into Wyoming. The NAA bastards tracked down over half of what was left of my tribe and exterminated them—women, children, sleeping in their tepees. We must stay in small roving groups now to survive—never staying in one place for more than a week or two, always leaving false trails. They have been sending out their search-and-destroy teams of choppers and tanks on a monthly basis. *You* tell us—that's why we called this meeting. Do *you* know of a way in—a way to destroy him once and for all? A way to avenge our people?"

Stone thought hard and looked down at the ground as if the answer might have been written in the hard dirt. He wasn't quite ready for all this. He had been close to being ant pâté about ten hours before—and now they were asking him questions of military strategy that Napoleon might have gotten a stomachache from.

"You say you have a person on the inside," Stone said without looking up as he got a sudden cramp in his neck and his gut started tightening with tension. He suddenly realized he wasn't going to get another moment's rest. He was going to be back in the fray—instantly. "What does he do—what's his rank."

"It's a woman," Meyra spoke up. "A friend of mine from high school from a nearby town who was recruited by the NAA about a year ago when they first started establishing their base. At first she hoped, as did many people in the territory, that they would be a positive force. But they weren't, and soon she saw that. But there's an unwritten policy of the NAA that they don't tell their recruits, Stone —and that is, no one leaves. Alive, anyway. So she met with me several times, relaying information to us about the state of things in there. We know where the main munitions are, the missile silo, even Patton's headquarters. But we just haven't felt we had the strength to mount a full attack."

"Do you have any explosives?" Stone asked, looking up so a sliver of sunlight caught him in the face and the entire band of Cheyenne could suddenly see just how badly Martin Stone had been beaten. Any lingering animosity they might have had toward the "white man" instantly vanished.

"Yes—some. We've saved up things we've taken from them. Don't think we've been doing nothing. We attacked several small convoys recently and have a truckload of weapons and ammunition. We made explosive detonators from bullets and attached them to a whole crate of antitank land mines—so they detonate on impact. They're heavy-duty."

"Then we've got to strike now," Stone said. "Immediately—tonight, in fact. I know what Patton's going to do—he's going to evacuate his base within twenty-four hours and send the ten-meg up, believing he'll have me trapped within its kill zone. This man is obsessed with my destruction. We must plan and mount an attack right now. Do you have any transportation?"

Little Bear pointed around to a clearing about twenty yards off, and Stone saw about a dozen or so three-wheelers, rough overland vehicles with thick tires that looked like they could just about climb the side of a mountain.

"My father rented 'em out—had a whole little business before the NAA killed him. But we managed to take out these before they came in a transport and carted away the rest. They're fast—and we've got automatic pistols wired up on both handles so they spit out a load of slugs as fast as you can pull the fucking trigger."

"Well, you tell me," Stone said, looking around the circle of denim-clad Cheyenne, some of them snapping their fingers as they listened to the music of their headphones and Stone simultaneously. "Do we go for it? I can't promise you that even one of you will come out of this alive—or that I will. But I know we're the last chance to stop that bastard before he launches."

They looked around at each other, then each one took out a long-bladed knife and stabbed it into the log between his legs.

"We're in, Stone," Little Bear said. "To victory—or the Great Happy Hunting Ground in the sky." Stone couldn't tell if he was mocking him or not.

CHAPTER

EIGHTEEN

A S THE sun fell from the sky behind the peaks of the Rockies off in the distance, a fleet of three-wheelers spread through the prairie that led to the general's fortified silo. They tore through the cacti and the groves of small, stumpy trees with ease, like porpoises through water. Ten Cheyenne and Martin Stone were all that stood in the way of the destruction of Colorado and the grinding of America under the murderous thumb of Patton. The colors of the sky slowly faded away, and they switched on their dimmed lights so thin beams fed out, pointed almost straight down, hardly visible from more than a hundred yards off.

Meyra rode in one of the all-terrain vehicles alongside Stone, keeping a wary eye on him. She had cleansed and salved his wounds, so only she among them knew how badly he had been hurt. She had given him an herbal powder to swallow, telling Stone that "It will almost make you feel like new tonight—tomorrow you'll tighten up and everything will hurt twice as much." But Stone gladly took the proffered substance. If there *was* a tomorrow, he'd be happy to suffer a little pain to see it. After an hour of riding the herb appeared to have helped tremendously, for his muscles seemed to move almost normally. He had a few broken fingers and toes, but Meyra had splinted them. And to his amazement Stone found his senses nearly functional—if not a hundred percent, then up there in high eighties. Even his swollen eye was half open now. It was nice to see the world again in stereo.

They had gone about ten miles, Stone slowly getting more and more used to the three-wheeler, so that he started curving around cacti, testing the vehicle's balance—as well as his own—when there was a set of headlights coming toward them from about a mile off. At Little Bear's command they all slowed to just a few miles per hour and switched off their lights. Stone searched frantically around on the dashboard of the thick-tired vehicle, as his was the only light that remained on, but after a few fumbling seconds he found the switch and slammed it off. The ten three-wheelers spread out so they formed a sort of half circle, hidden behind vegetation and cacti. Stone found himself a niche of cover at the right end of the line and sat there in the slung-back seat, drowning in the thick black bear coat he wore, his finger resting on one of the triggers of his twin 9-mm autopistols that they all had mounted. The thing looked sort of makeshift, and Stone wondered if it would actually work—all held in place with wire and duct tape. But he had other firearms as well, tucked away beneath the engulfing fur. The Cheyenne had let him go through their munitions truck, and he had selected an H&K 9-mm with 10-shot clip and an old U.S. Army Service .45 that looked like it had been through World War II. He had tested the well-worn weapon; it had worked just fine and had been a lot more accurate than a lot of later model .45s that he had fired. He kept his hand on the handlebars but opened the coat for instant access just in case.

It didn't take long for the NAA patrol jeep with a back-mounted machine gun to find them. And when they did, they wished they hadn't. For the Cheyenne let the jeep move right into the trap. And when the prey was caught, they opened up from all sides. The three soldiers in the vehicle barely knew what hit them as the silencer-equipped autopistols burped out a whole wall of firepower. There were but sharp little sounds as if hundreds of small animals were whispering at once. And when the whispers stopped after a few seconds, three bodies tumbled out onto the ground, riddled with dozens of holes, blood pouring out like fountains from every one.

Without a word Little Bear started up his cross-country vehicle again, and the rest followed suit. Within seconds they were moving forward. Stone felt slightly more confident. He hadn't really believed inside of himself that these guys could really do it. But they could. Perhaps they actually had a fucking chance, though he wouldn't have bet the bunker on it.

The two guards atop machine-gun towers at the eastern side of the fort about a hundred yards apart from each other yelled back and forth. They had heard that Patton was pulling them all out in the morning, and behind them, in the center of the two-hundred-man fortress whose sole purpose was to guard the missile in its midst, there were all kinds of activities going on—trucks being loaded, supplies being girded up. The two guards stood in little wooden boxes, like something a kid might build as a tree house—and not much better made—about forty feet above the ground. The towers ringed the half-mile-wide fort with its steel-mesh fence, Patton's standard defensive fortifications for all his bases.

"What do you think?" one of them screamed out to the other, cupping his hands into a flesh megaphone. "I heard we're going to be sent South again—maybe even into New Mexico."

"Son of a bitch," the other yelled back through the dark

night air, the moon hidden behind clouds like a low-watt light bulb at the far end of a basement. "I can't even tell you what I think." But he wanted to relay his information, so he screamed out what to him were hints and therefore more acceptable should any of the general's Elite Corps officers hear. "The A-thing, you know. The *M*." What he meant were the atomic device, the missile, but the other guard hadn't the faintest idea what he was talking about.

"What the fuck are you—" He never got to finish the question. An arrow ripped into his throat and clean through the back of his neck. The guard threw his hands around the arrow with a look of infinite horror on his suddenly pain-racked face and tried to pull it out. But as it started to come free, the backward-angled hunting arrowhead pulled into the back of his neck, just ripping more veins and nerves to shreds. He stumbled backward and then tumbled right over the yard-high wall of the tower. The body spun end over end and crashed to the dirt with a wet sound.

The second guard could hardly make out what was happening in the dark. There were supposed to be searchlights at every tower, but things had gotten tough lately, and supplies were limited. The nearest spotlight was three towers away. He lifted his binoculars and had just sighted up the other man as he started his fall to the ground when another silent Cheyenne arrow whispered a good hundred yards from behind a boulder. The NAA'er took the yard-long arrow through the side, slicing right between his ribs. The razor-sharp head sliced into the bottom part of the heart, cutting it in two. The heart literally exploded in his chest as if a bomb had gone off, and blood poured out of his mouth and eyes and nose in a violent spray of red. The body spun around three times, as if doing some kind of insane little dance, and then fell to the floor. Somehow it slid through the trapdoor that led to the stairs and managed to tumble nearly halfway down them, flopping wildly along the metal steps, leaving a trail of red from top to bottom. Then the corpse came to a rest, its feet caught between two steps so that it hung beneath the stairs upside down, like a deer being bled.

The three-wheelers bolted from the darkness and up to the gate. The double mufflers they had installed made the things about as quiet as a gasoline-powered motor vehicle could get, and with the noise floating toward them from the far end of the fort, they could hardly be heard beyond a few-hundred-foot radius. One of the Indians jumped from his all-terrain vehicle and was at the padlocked gate in a flash. He took something from his pocket, slapped it onto the huge lock, and stepped back, turning his head. There was a muffled pop and a little cloud of white smoke that quickly dissipated. The Cheyenne just touched the lock, and it fell to the ground in pieces. He pushed open the gate, which swung all the way back, and jumped back onto his bike. They were in.

The attack unit immediately split up into the three squads, each composed of three men—one group to take out the munitions depot, one to try to find and kill Patton, and the third to rove around the camp wreaking havoc, keeping them off-balance, so they wouldn't even know where the attack was coming from. They were also to try to locate and release Stone's men, who might tip the balance enough to win the battle, especially if they could get to their tanks. Stone, Meyra, and Little Bull would take the silo. They'd all use bows and silenced autopistols—try to stay as quiet as possible until the shit hit the fan. At least, such was the plan.

But plans have a nasty habit of falling apart the moment they're hatched, for Stone, Little Bear, and Meyra had hardly gone a hundred feet or so into the fort, along a narrow street between long rows of supply dumps, when they heard a sound that Stone didn't like at all: the sound of a man counting down from ten. A firing squad. And there was only one bunch of people Patton would be killing off now—what was left of Stone's teams. The words were coming from behind a wall of truck tires a good ten feet high, and Stone could hear that the officer was down to eight. Stone motioned frantically over at the wall, and the Cheyenne followed him over so that their three-wheelers slammed right into the base of the thing. They were off and up the big rubber doughnuts, climbing to the top in a flash. Stone reached the top first and lay flat on the tops of two side-by-side stacks of tires.

His men were directly across from him, staring back at the squad of men who were about to do them in with the most fearless looks they could muster, though most of their eyes were moist. Stone's men were young, had hardly lived. None of them wanted to go. And then Stone saw something that filled his heart with an electric jolt of joy—the dog, Excaliber, sitting on his hind legs, with a somber, resigned look on his muzzle. His front right leg was covered with blood and looked to be at an odd angle. The pitbull must have gotten hurt when Stone's tank was taken. And the bastards hadn't even splinted it or anything. Just put him against the wall, along with the rest of them. Stone looked quickly down, and right below him, almost close enough to touch, were a firing squad of ten men. Five of them stood straight, the other five in a row just in front of them, kneeling. All held their M16s straight out, waiting for the magic number to be reached.

"Four, three . . ." the officer went on, standing by the side, his hand raised up, ready to descend like a guillotine. There was no time. Stone lifted both of the impact-capped land mines he was holding and, rising to his knees, flung one of them in each direction, like ten-pound Frisbees. He screamed to his men to duck and then fell backward onto the tires just as the two Cheyenne were coming up. Stone somehow grabbed hold of both of them as he tumbled back so that he took them with him. And barely in time. There was a great roar that seemed to go off just beneath their feet, as if the earth itself were erupting upward. Then a flash of yellow and orange that blinded them temporarily, so that everything was just a blinking orb of light. The entire wall of tires seemed to slowly tilt away from the explosion, and they felt they were all in a dream, almost as if they were floating. And then everything speeded up and the tires crashed forward and down onto the ground, sending them flying as huge truck wheels bounced off in every direction.

Stone was the first to his feet, his eyes still having difficulty adjusting to the dimness of the night. He leapt forward, jumping across some of the sprawled tires and could see enough to know that it had worked. The land mines were meant to take out vehicles, tanks, not men. They had been torn to ribbons, pieces of them sprayed around the place as if they had gone through a grinder. Not one of them moved. He raised his head and started forward through the still dissipating smoke, anxious that his own men might have met the same fate. But they were rising already, groaning, some with busted eardrums and burned legs and back, but all were alive. Stone counted six. So two more had died in the tank attack.

"It's Stone," Bo shouted out, a trickle of blood running from the corner of his mouth. But he was smiling. They all were. Excaliber rushed up to him, his tongue trailing out of his mouth like a big pink rug. He hobbled along on three legs, though he moved fairly well considering, and slammed his head into Stone's leg, butting him again and again in thanks. The belief that it had in fact picked the right master was confirmed forever as far as the terrier was concerned. Even Bull rose and gave Stone a big grin. Now that Stone knew the man he had suspected all along had not in fact been the traitor among them, he felt guilty and totally different toward the rough, but well-intentioned, fighter. Stone held out his hand, and Bull took it as the remainder of the attack force gathered around them, all reaching out to touch the son of a bitch who had just snatched them from the very drooling jaws of death.

"He'd gotten to three," Bo said, slapping Stone on the shoulder for the third time.

"Two—I think it was two," a voice said as the two Cheyenne dropped down. The men reached for nonexistent weapons at their sides, but Stone reassured them that the Indians were friends. With the explosions of the land mines the rest of the fort knew something was up. Stone had blown their silence trip within about twenty seconds. But then he'd had no choice. They'd just have to change the screenplay a little in mid-shooting.

"Look, do you know where the tanks were taken?" Stone asked them all frantically.

"I—I think I overheard a guard say they were in C Warehouse, whatever that means," Bull said as he shook his head, trying to clear out the loose screws and cobwebs that the detonation of the land mines had created.

"Yes, I know where that is," Little Bear said, looking around nervously when he heard a sound come from nearby. He extracted a snub-nosed .44 from his black denim jacket and held it ready. "But perhaps you could take any of them. From what I know, mostly what they use here is Bradley IIIs. Probably getting ready to take out of here over in Section D, north end of the fort." He pointed off to the distance where they could now hear firing, as the rest of the Cheyenne attack units were obviously running into opposition now that the fort had been alerted. The loud, crisp pops of the land mines going off here and there meant they were already using their heaviest firepower.

"We gotta move," Stone said, addressing them all. They were ready to follow just about any fucking order he had to give them now. The fucking guy had come through. He saw them staring at him with near hero worship in their eyes, and he looked down, embarrassed, as he spoke. "Look, there's no time for plans—just try to take whatever tank or tanks you can and stir the place up. Then get the hell out of here. Head due east—you hear me?—due east."

They all looked at one another for a second, knowing it was the last time they might ever see each other. And then they split up, moving fast in all directions.

CHAPTER

NINETEEN

S TONE AND the two Cheyenne flew through the back alleys and narrow passages between the barracks, the rows of canisters, and parts that filled the place. Excaliber had somehow fitted himself alongside Stone in the slung-back seat of the three-wheeler, but there wasn't a hell of a lot of room, so he kept digging into Stone's leg, trying to get more space, the front part of him half hanging out of the tearing vehicle. At last they emerged from the darkness and into the light. And the silo came into view. The chrome-topped hood rose out of the ground a good six feet and was perhaps ten feet wide. Four floodlights sent down brilliant beams of light that made the place well lit enough to shoot a movie.

The three all-terrain vehicles pulled to a stop just where the darkness turned to light and hid the three-wheelers in the shadows. They started forward in a half crouch, Excaliber sort of crawling along behind when a voice stopped them in their tracks and a figure stepped forward from behind a shed.

"Stone, Stone, always so predictable," the general mock scolded the man he hated most in this world. "Now how did I know you were going to come to this silo?"

"Just psychic, I guess," Stone muttered back as he noted from the periphery of his vision that the low roofs of two of the barracks had machine-gun posts, two of them—both aimed at the intruders. "But then you're a very talented man when it comes to murder. The whole world knows that." Stone smirked, trying to rile the bastard a little. Trying to follow his father's constant adage to always make your opponent angry, lose control. For then you can take advantage of his impulsive motion or action—and destroy him.

But the general, unlike Stone, took the ability to kill well and in large numbers as a compliment and smiled back. "Thank you. I appreciate the kind words. But, Mr. Stone, there is one thing—before I kill you. Your little Rin Tin Tin there killed my favorite dog—if you remember. Now I have another dog that would like to meet him. A close friend of Apollo's, rest his soul." The general clapped his hands hard twice, and the sharp retorts bounced around the nearby walls, and out of nowhere a pitbull emerged, coming straight to the general's side. He was huge, the biggest of the breed that Stone had ever seen, and Excaliber was no slouch in that department, either, weighing in at over eighty-five the last time Stone had put him on the bunker scale. But this bruiser who stood at shoulder height, perhaps as large as a Doberman, had to tip the scales at a hundred and fifty. It must have been a mutated gene of some sort, from the radiation that lingered throughout America. But if it was a mutant, the animal in no way looked imperfect. As both Stone and Excaliber looked across at their opposite numbers who stood at the far side of the silo, they could see that the canine was in perfect shape, with muscles that literally rippled across every square inch of its body, even as it breathed. Its neck was as thick as a man's thigh, and its long jaws hung open slightly, revealing incisors a good six inches long that looked like they could snap through steel.

"A final bet," Patton said, sweeping his hand across the fort, the missile silo. "You know I'm a betting man. Always have been. To me God tells you how he feels in a bet. After all, it's up to him, right? So it's my dog against yours, Stone—winner takes everything. And I mean everything."

"No way, Patton," Stone began to yell back at the sadistic bastard. "Excaliber's front leg doesn't even work, he's wounded, infected . . . he's—" Stone looked down at the hapless dog, which didn't look too happy about the turn of events, either. As a fighting dog bred to kill tigers, he was always ready for a good scrap. But the very thing that had made his breed so fierce and indestructible, aside from their cannonball bodies and jaws that were more powerful than any other dog's in the world, was their intelligence. So the pitbull was also a realist. In good shape, he knew he could kick the other mutt's ass. But his paw being useless and hanging in front of him, Excaliber knew he was in for trouble, big trouble.

"You don't understand, Stone." Patton laughed as he stepped back and held out his hands. "You don't have a choice. Go, Aristophanes, kill." He clapped his hands once, and the huge pitbull lunged forward, its jaws opened and snarling like a wolf. "Nor does your dog," he added, but no one even heard that. If Patton had named his dogs after Greek poets and philosophers to point out a softer, more refined side of their nature, this one hadn't been told about it. He looked mean and real bad.

Excaliber rolled his eyes up at Stone with an oh-God-do-I-really-have-to-do-this kind of expression. And then he charged forward to meet the other pitbull, which was just passing the silo itself, halfway to him. He tried to charge, anyway. Excaliber made two full strides forward and then collapsed straight down on his right side as his leg buckled out from under him. All things considered, this was just about the best thing that could have happened to him. For right where his skull had just been, the adversary slammed its jaws shut with such force that a tooth broke free from the inner part of its mouth and flew out. Excaliber, lying flat on his face in the dust, saw the leg of the attacker just inches from his own mouth, and being an opportunistic kind of creature, he just sort of opened up his jaws without even rising and slid his head suddenly forward like a snake striking. The teeth crunched into the animal's left front leg, cracking it at mid-joint with a loud snapping sound. Aristophanes fell down in a heap, cracking the underside of his jaw, and Excaliber pulled away until he was about two yards off and crouching down, growling with a high-pitched squeal like a steampipe going off.

Stone and the two Cheyenne watched, their hands primed to grab for their weapons. For they knew that whatever happened, the machine gunners on the roof would open up the second it was over, the second Patton commanded them to. So they watched with both fascination and horror, along with the rest of them, as the two animals battled to the death.

Excaliber was feeling a hell of a lot better already, now that he had taken out the opponent's leg. That made the odds at least slightly better, and the canine knew that the other would be awkward at first while it had been walking on three legs for nearly two days. It waited patiently, crouched back on its back legs, waiting for the enemy to strike, to make a mistake. The pitbull didn't have to wait long. Aristophanes rose with a howl of rage from his rough tumble to the ground. He turned, mindless of the pain in his leg, and started forward, slowly at first, as if to lull Excaliber into thinking he was going to circle—and then suddenly sprang up off both back legs. But the smaller pitbull had been thinking the other was about to try such an attack. As the immense killer dog came soaring through the air like a rocket ready to draw blood, Excaliber pushed himself over, so he went onto his back. Aristophanes soared right over his head, snapping down at him, perhaps inches away. But the bites missed, and the smaller dog kicked its rear legs up, helping the airborne attacker along.

Patton's dog, an animal that had fought fifty fights in its three-year career, had never lost one. It knew it was tough. So it had no fear, took no caution, even with three legs. Excaliber twisted himself upright with a single whiplike twist of his strong body. He came up to three legs and faced the enemy, which was still adjusting itself after its ten-foot flight, then crash-landing on its head on a small rock. Aristophanes let out a roar of fury, a sound that should have come from a lion or a mountain cat rather than a dog, a high-pitched wail of pure rage. He came forward on the fly, once again not judging the strength of the broken leg. He was almost upon Excaliber when he went down again, his jaws snapping, this time into the dirt so that his teeth scooped up a whole mound of earth that was swept into his mouth and throat. Excaliber again took advantage of whatever presented itself to him. In this case it was his opponent's stomach as the animal lay sideways for an instant before it could regain its balance. The smaller pitbull snapped forward, digging in as far as it could, and closed its own murderous jaws. The teeth dug deep into the animal's guts, deep inside it, ripping through intestine and kidney, liver and spleen. Excaliber clenched once again, hard, and then ripped away with all his might.

The flood of guts and innards, coated in a slime of blood that exploded out as Excaliber pulled backward, was truly revolting to see. The only one that didn't know it was dead was Aristophanes itself, which somehow hobbled to its three working legs and stared at Excaliber, pulling its lips back, snarling, showing what remained of its macho. It felt strange, like everything was tingling, and its stomach felt on fire, but there was no time to stop now—it would see later. It started toward Excaliber again and tried once more to leap, to propel itself like a missile. But nothing happened. The legs collapsed like rotten, splintered pieces of wood, and the huge pitbull, dragging a trail of intestine along with it, sort of slithered toward Excaliber, still opening and closing its jaws in a frenzy.

Even the victorious Excaliber couldn't stand the pitiful sight. The dog had been brave; it fought to the end. It didn't deserve to suffer. Knowing he had won already, but having his own streak of animal compassion, Excaliber lunged suddenly forward and clamped onto the dying canine's throat. With a single powerful snap and then a shake of his muscular head, he flung the once powerful animal out of his jaws again, and it fell to the ground, dead.

Stone and the two Cheyenne moved almost instantaneously the instant they saw Aristophanes receive the coup de grace. And barely in time, for the machine gunners above them clicked back their firing mechanisms and pulled their triggers. But the attackers were already rushing to each side, heaving up the land mines they carried in satchels around their shoulders. Four streams of .30-caliber slugs scissored patterns all over the field, sending up numerous puffs of smoke and digging little pockmocks into the hard dirt. Stone heaved first one mine to the left, the other to the right, spinning them both out like discuses at the Olympics. To each side of him he could see the Cheyenne throw theirs, and then they all dived down again as the lines of bullets came screaming toward them. Explosion after explosion ripped the air, as if lightning bolts were striking all around them. NAA troops went flying from both rooftops, spinning wildly, arms and legs flailing around like broken dolls. It was truly—as the lyrics went—raining men.

CHAPTER
TWENTY

W HEN THE smoke had cleared and the few screams had died out, as had their screamers, Stone jumped up with his .45 in hand and spun around to sight up Patton. But the general was already gone, dust swirling where he had stood. Stone instantly shifted his eyes down to the dog, praying that after such a valiant and clever fight it had survived. But the pitbull was already rising and shaking itself from head to foot. Although coated with a layer of dust from the mine explosions and a few splashes of blood from the dog it had sent to the Great Pound in the Sky, the ass-kicking canine seemed okay. In the sudden, immediate silence Stone could hear the cracking of firearms from every direction of the fort, along with larger explosions, grenades, artillery. All hell was breaking loose, though there was not the slightest way of knowing what was happening or who was winning.

Stone rushed forward, stepping over some of the ripped bodies, and reached the shining surface of the silo's cover.

He ran his hand down the outside; it was as smooth as glass and as tough as shit, Stone knew. Yet they had to get in there and fast.

"Here," Little Bear said, taking two more mines from his satchel. "These have ten-second timers. They'll go off together." He slammed the mines onto the crease of the silo cone, the razor-thin line that separated the two halves of titanium steel, and turned a little dial.

"Move," the Cheyenne yelled, and the three of them, with Excaliber hobbling along gamely on three legs, beat a quick retreat behind a pile of thick lumber planking some fifty feet to the side and barely made it when the two mines went off with a roar. They poked their heads out again and, seeing the smoke drifting up, rushed back to the chromium cap. But aside from scraping things up here and there and gouging a few shallow little craters in the surface, no real damage had been done whatsoever. The silo hadn't opened an inch.

The three of them, with the dog licking at its broken leg, stood motionless in front of the silo, totally stymied at how to get inside. It was as if the entire journey, the men who had died in battle, the ordeal they had all just been through, was all for naught—stopped cold in their tracks at the last few inches. Stone bent down as the dog looked up at him with pain-racked eyes.

"Sorry, pal," he said, getting down on one knee and lifting the damaged leg gently in both hands. The dog groaned slightly, letting out a little half-stifled yip of pain and then let Stone handle the leg, looking with interest as his master began examining it. Stone couldn't see any bones poking through anywhere, nor any blood. But the bone was clearly cracked, the bottom half of the leg going off at perhaps a five-degree angle from the top half. The whole thing must have just been held in place by the tendons and muscles that surrounded it, Stone realized. It was only because the goddamn pitbull was made of steel inside, as well as out, that it had been able to go on, to fight, to kill, using a broken appendage. Stone patted the animal on the head.

"This is going to hurt you a hell of a lot more than me, you hear," Stone said. Excaliber looked at him trustingly, knowing his master was doing some strange human thing to his leg that would make it all better. A jolt of pain suddenly surged through the dog that taxed even its unflappable nervous system as Stone pulled the bottom part of the leg back into place and snapped the two parts cleanly together. The dog howled several times, holding its head high as if baying at the invisible moon. But he let Stone handle it, kept his paw on his master's knee, motionless. Stone made a quick but sturdy splint from several straight pieces of metal he found—shrapnel from the exploding machine-gun nests— about as long as pencils. He held them parallel on each side of the break and then took shoelaces from some combat boots nearby, whose owner no longer needed them and tied the metal holding the whole thing firmly in place. The dog put its weight down when he was at last done and walked around a few steps as if testing it. Then it looked up at Stone and barked, and its tongue rolled out from its jaws, again in its usual happy-go-lucky state.

Stone had scarcely risen from setting Excaliber's bone and turned to ask Little Bear what suggestions he might have for penetrating the silo when he heard a sudden deep vibration, and the very ground beneath their feet shook as if they were in the grip of a small earthquake. Stone knew instantly what the sound was. He experienced it just days before. The noises of the missile's systems being turned on, of the mechanism for the silo's protective hood being opened. And sure enough, as the three of them jerked their heads around toward the sound, the chromium cover moved and began sliding back with a deep hum. Stone rushed toward the missile hole and stared down as the cover dropped farther out of the way and into deep slots on each side of the cylindrical launch tube. Little Bear and Meyra came alongside him, and the Cheyenne chief whistled.

"I've never really seen one of these motherfuckers—except, you know, in *Time* magazine or something. It's big." He leaned all the way forward as the silo covers dropped completely out of sight on each side of them so there was just a ten-foot-wide, hundred-fifty-foot deep hole below them with a missile taking up over half that height. Far below they could suddenly see little spits of white-hot fire start to lick out of the tail.

"We've got to stop it," Stone screamed. "Somehow." He turned to the Cheyenne and grabbed him frantically by the lapels of his denim jacket. "Do you have any more mines . . . anything? Anything we can throw down there and—" Little Bear pulled away from Stone's grip, giving the white man a strange look as he reached for the satchel hanging behind him. There were three left. He took them out and held them stacked in his arms.

"These are impact," the Cheyenne said coolly. "No time to get away. Throw—and bang."

"Then I'll take one," Stone said, meeting the Indian's questioning gaze.

"And me too," Meyra said, reaching out for the third one before either of them could stop her. They pulled them back in their arms to heave them down into the chemical-smelling hole beneath their feet as the flame of the rocket seemed to grow brighter.

"No, wait," Meyra suddenly screamed out as her eyes caught a figure rushing up the curved metal stairway that ran up around the inside of the silo. "It's Carla, our contact. She's risked her life for us—we've got to let her get out." Stone groaned and looked up at the sky, which returned no advice. He dropped his arm and leaned over to look into the mist-shrouded chamber.

"Get the fuck up here. You hear me. We're dropping bombs down there in ten seconds. Ten seconds." The woman seemed to speed up, though she stumbled here and there as she carried a device about as large as a suitcase. "One," Stone screamed down into the hole, so that his voice echoed back and forth even above the growing roar of the rocket's ignition system. Carla speeded up even more, and Stone kept counting all the way, goosing her along. He could see that the timing on all this was going to be so close as to be ridiculous. The whole perfectly sculpted missile of mega-destruction was already beginning to vibrate and prepare its computer system for takeoff.

Suddenly she was right at the top, and Little Bear reached out hands to help her out. "Run," he said, pointing toward the lumber pile and, without stopping, she rushed on. The three of them looked at each other—wanting to time their throws perfectly so all three land mines went off simultaneously instead of just blowing each other out of existence. They all knew the blasts would be so quick that they would be caught in at least some of the force. But as the missile suddenly roared into flame below them, lighting up the whole missile silo like a Roman candle, they knew they'd run out of time.

Three arms flung their explosive packets of steel forward, and three bodies pushed themselves backward. If they hadn't already been moving in a direction completely away from the explosion that instantly occurred, they surely would have been killed. For suddenly the cylindrical hole in the earth roared out a pillar of fire that rose straight up in the air a good three hundred feet. All three land mines came down within feet of each other at the very base of the rocket. As they went off, the brunt of their explosions were reflected up from the concrete launchpad and into the engine section of the ICBM. The entire liquid fuel system ignited at once, as the fuel tanks ruptured, and the flames of the rocket exhaust sent the whole thing up like a funeral pyre.

The explosion was so great that it could be felt for up to ten miles. Animals and peasants in their slovenly huts all stopped what they were doing and turned their heads toward the sound, feeling the vibrations in their feet and bones. Then they turned away again and went on with their respective tasks. Whoever had died, it wasn't them.

But for Stone, and the two Cheyenne, it was like being in the center of a tornado, and they felt themselves literally lifted up and flung backward through the air like dead leaves, flipping and spinning around. For one mad second Stone was flung back in his mind to when he had been a child at the beach in California riding the surf and he had been caught in a wave, and the spinning ocean waters had spun and twisted him around like this. He had thought for a few seconds that he was going to die. And again the same claustrophobic panic swept through him of not even knowing where he was—the sky and earth spinning around unrecognizably. But as he came down hard nearly thirty feet from where he had started, Stone's mind was riveted back to the present by the waves of pain that slammed through his already ready-for-collection-by-the-Salvation-Army wreck of a body.

The roar of the rising flame of pure white slammed into his ears like the scream of a jet engine next to his head. And as he lay on his side in a daze, the flame already began to lower slightly and the thundering roar of the fire subsided to about half its height. The missile had burned over half its fuel out in one titanic explosion; now it would burn slowly for days, lower and lower until like a candle it went out in its own wax. What all this would do to the radioactive core of the missile Stone couldn't begin to imagine, nor did he try.

The cold dirt that he suddenly became aware of in his mouth brought him back to total awareness, and Stone opened his eyes wide, coughing out the foul, chemical-tasting soil. He rolled over just in time to see a helicopter fly overhead. It seemed to hover over them about two hundred feet up, just out of the line of the rising pillar of fire and smoke, seemed to try to find them. And then suddenly it shot forward, curving around in a wide circle so that it was quickly heading north.

Stone rose shakily to his feet, as did the others. Excaliber, who had been far back from the explosion, walked on a fast three-legged hobble over to Stone and nipped at his leg with concern.

"It's Patton," Carla, the female tech who had barely escaped from the silo, said as she came forward, holding the strange, high-tech mechanical device out in front of her. "Up in that chopper. I know it—it's his private craft."

"So he got away," Stone said, turning to her and seeing that she was quite attractive, despite hair severely cut back in military fashion. She wore a white technician's smock and low pumps and looked terrified. "At least we got the missile," Stone said with a tired sigh. "That thing ain't going nowhere. At least we bought just a little time."

"You don't understand," Carla said with tears forming in her eyes. "There's another one just ten miles north of here —armed and ready. That's where Patton's gone, I know it. You haven't bought time—just minutes."

CHAPTER

TWENTY-ONE

"JESUS FUCKING Christ," Stone said, his face growing as pale as a Ku Klux Klanner's freshly laundered sheet.

"I've got to get my men the hell out of here," Little Bear said, his own coppery tones going to the chalky end of the color chart. He whipped out a small, fat pistol from behind his belt and raised it straight up in the air. He pulled the trigger, and a rocketlike shell rose rapidly about two hundred feet up, trailing a thin white stream. Suddenly it burst and lit up in a star pattern off to the side of the still burning missile silo.

Within about five minutes, six of the three-wheelers showed up, along with both tanks that had been captured from Stone's force. His men had taken them back again, Stone was proud to see, as they came toward the silo, battle-scarred, but treads still turning, still grinding on. A line of the all-terrain vehicles and the tanks pulled to a stop in front of Stone, and heads popped up from the turrets of the Bradleys.

"There's no time to bullshit or congratulate ourselves," Stone yelled at the top of his lungs, standing on the seat of his three-wheeler, which he had dragged out from the shadows. "Patton has escaped and there's a missile coming at us—right now. We don't have a chance in hell, but we've gotta try. Don't wait up for anyone if they falter. Go straight south. If you find a mountain or a high dirt rise, hide. And whatever you do, don't get caught in the direct blast or—"

"Good luck, you bastards," Stone yelled out to them as he started to slide down into the three-wheeled vehicle. "It's been a privilege to fight alongside every one of you—" But the last few words got drowned out as the motors started up again in a roar, as if a drag race was about to take place. And it was. The three-wheelers and the tanks tore ass away from the flaming wreckage of the silo. All around them, fires rose from the damage the twin attack forces had caused, secondaries still going off from time to time and sending up big fountains of glowing shrapnel and smoke high into the night air.

Part of the steel-mesh, barbed-wire-topped gate was still standing at the southern end of the fort, and the three-wheelers slowed down as they let the tanks slam through, their heavy bodies flattening the poles, their treads grinding the mesh into broken wire beneath them. Stone rode in the tri-bike he had come in. He was happy to see that his Harley was still up on the back of the tank he had been commanding. Not that it was too likely he'd ever get to use the fucking thing again. Excaliber rode crunched down in the seat alongside him. And in the nearest three-wheeler, driven by Little Bear, Carla was squeezed in tight, madly fiddling with the many controls of the device she had expended so much energy to save. They drove out of the fort and across the prairie, the three-wheelers turning on their headlights to full magnitude, as there was no one to hide from anymore. Except an atomic missile. And that didn't need too many clues to find them.

They drove for miles, all of them looking up every minute or so, glancing over their shoulders. They were being pursued by death itself, no ifs, ands, or buts. The tension was unbearable. A race against time, only they had no idea how long the contest would last—or what the outcome would be. So they just drove their asses off, the tri-bikes pulling slightly ahead of the two tanks, which moved about five miles per hour slower at thirty-five.

Stone kept noticing Carla playing with her machine as it lit up here and there and let out a few beeps that he could hear, even while riding ten feet to the side.

"What the hell is that?" Stone yelled over, above the roar of the fleet of vehicles.

She couldn't hear and wrinkled up her face to show it, but Little Bear had, and he said to her in exactly the same phrasing Stone had used, "He wants to know, what the hell is that?"

"It's an—MTO, a missile trajectory overrider," she said, stuttering nervously, hardly able to work the thing and hang on to her minute amount of space next to the Cheyenne at the same time.

"She says it's a missile something overrider," Little Bear shouted back at Stone with something approaching a grin on his usually inscrutable face. "Just what we need."

"What the hell is a missile overrider?" Stone screamed back, steering a little closer to the other vehicle until they were tearing along side by side near the back of the pack of the all-terrains but a good fifty yards ahead of the two tanks.

"He says, what the hell is a missile overrider?" Little Bear yelled at the woman, though she sat only inches away.

"It overrides missile commands," she answered, hitting at the machine as she tried to make it respond to her commands, which up until then it hadn't been doing. "It's experimental," she went on. The Indian looked at her as if she were slightly mad. "I can't promise it will work—or even that I can make it work. But if I can, then it could . . ." She trailed off into mumbles as she started working at the complex-looking portable device again, trying to get the right sequences of commands to make it operational.

"She says . . ." Little Bear started to yell, turning to Stone. "Oh shit, I don't know what the fuck she's talking about," the Cheyenne said, waving his hand at her as if she were perhaps slightly cracked. "I don't think she knows, either," he added, cupping one hand over his mouth so she couldn't hear. Which she didn't, but it hardly mattered, since she knew, as none of them did, that what she was doing would determine whether or not they lived beyond the next ten minutes.

It didn't even take that long for the moment of truth to arrive. Excaliber was the first to sense it. Stone felt the animal jump around on the seat beside him. Then its paws were up on his shoulder so that it was standing almost straight up on its hind legs, its muzzle pointing up at the sky in a hunting posture. Stone slowed the all-terrain slightly and twisted his head around. He felt his heart tighten up into a nice tight little ball about the size of a BB, for the missile was coming straight down on them. It was clearly visible, as big as a match head, leaving a long, thin trail behind it across the night sky, a little tongue of fire spitting out behind. It was coming from due north and at the angle that it was descending from, about ten thousand feet, it would go off just about between their eyes. Within seconds the rest of the crew saw it, too, the Cheyenne fighters twisting around and looking with horrified eyes, the tanks in the rear being warned by numerous built-in defensive systems that they were being tracked by a radar signal. They knew—every one of them— that they were about to be consumed in atomic fire, their bodies turned into atoms screaming off at the speed of light.

They each prayed to their own private god, and those who had no gods wished that they did.

"Stop!" Carla suddenly screamed out to Little Bear. "Let me at least try to use this thing. We're not going to outrun the bomb now—that's for sure." She looked up and saw it starting its long, slow descent, as if it had all the time in the world. One always came late to one's own party.

"All right, all right," the Cheyenne screamed back in frustration at being able to do nothing about his demise. He slammed the brakes on, and she almost fell out of the thing, jamming her feet forward and wedging herself in. She jumped from the three-wheeler and set the beeping, blinking device down on the ground. With both hands able to work on the thing, she suddenly clicked the right sequence in. Saying a quick prayer and crossing herself, she pressed the "Command Override" button. Carla stared up at the sky, her eyes again filling with tears. She just couldn't help it. She wanted to be brave, but she didn't feel that way at all. Not at all.

Nothing seemed to happen—at first. The missile was definitely descending, making a long curve from the left like a jet coming in for a landing. Now they could actually see its fins, the size of the warhead that was about to detach itself. But as the entire crew stopped in their tracks and looked up, the missile suddenly seemed to pour on a little extra flame. The ICBM kept curving over them, then past them. Now it was rising again, definitely rising, going higher up by the second and curving all the way around so that it had completed a 180-degree turn. It was headed back north—back where it had hatched.

The men cheered, standing on their vehicles, the Indians screaming out sharp Cheyenne war cries, the tank boys rebel yells. But it all meant the same thing. Their assholes were still attached to their asses, which, all things considered, was doing pretty good.

"We can't rest," Carla said, standing up and lurching over

as if she were about to vomit. She collapsed in the seat next to Little Bear. "I couldn't direct it far," she said, holding her head in her hands as if the pressure were about to make her collapse.

"All I could do is send it back toward its originating command signal. That's about twenty miles north of here. We're still going to get caught in the blast. Go, go, go—make this thing go, will you?" She burst into tears and bent forward so that her head was between her legs. But they had all heard the outburst, and smiles quickly turned to frightened expressions as they threw the many vehicles into gear and, tires and treads squealing out dust from beneath them, they shot forward like rocket cars. There was no tomorrow and they drove like it—with utter disregard for life or limb. The all-terrain vehicles hit speeds up to fifty, flying up into the air sometimes as they went over bumps, barely skirting cacti that reached out with long spikes. The tanks hit forty, then forty-five miles per hour, everything inside being thrown around as if they were in an earthquake, all the dials and panel lights blinking, warnings of every kind going off as if the tank was screaming at them to get the fuck out of there.

Bull, in one of the Bradleys, saw it first, using the tank's long-range sighting equipment—a drop-off ahead about two miles to the left. It would be worth heading for, as his long-range radar showed the decline to be at least twenty feet. He radioed to the other tank, and they each sent a man up to yell down to the Cheyenne and Stone what was up. The fighting column swung to the left, following Bull, who guided the way using the electronics of the Bradley. Then, as they came out of a thick grove of cacti, the tanks rolling over most of the smaller ones, they were suddenly looking out over an almost barren terrain and the sudden and steep drop-off to it—about a hundred yards off. From the closer vantage point they could now see that it was, or had been, a highway. An interstate with raised, four-lane concrete roadway that had been built right along the edge of the thirty-mile-long rift in the earth running east to west. Now the highway was just an obsolete relic, collapsed, broken down everywhere like a child's fallen house of cards. But even in its disintegration it might help them, shield them—if they could get to the other side.

The fleet made for the cracked highway, every man now accelerating for his own ass, the vehicles tearing along like they were coming in on the finish line at the Indianapolis 500. They spread out in a long line, approaching the highway and the drop beyond from different angles and speeds. Stone took his all-terrain to the limit, pushing and pulling every fucking thing that made it go, and the engine screamed out in protest but seemed to shoot forward an inch or two faster. He reached the edge of the interstate and felt his heart speed up, for it suddenly looked like a lot deeper drop on the other side than he had thought. Stone slapped the dog on the head, warning it to hold on tight and then set his own body.

The three-wheeled vehicle shot across the cracked four-laner and then right over the edge of the precipitous drop in the earth as if going off a ski jump. It soared through the air over huge chunks of jagged concrete set in the white, grainy sand below. Stone swore he was airborne forever and thought he could see other three-wheelers flying wildly around him. Then the ground was coming up fast and they hit—hard. Somehow Stone hung on to the vehicle with every bit of strength in his clenched fists and brought it to a reeling stop, the pitbull slamming up against him. Stone wheeled the oil-smoking three-wheeler around and searched for the others.

They were flying over the edge of the highway one after another, steel lemmings leaping in ungraceful, wheel-spinning arcs into the rocks and the dirt below. As his eyes scanned across the bizarre airborne fleet, Stone's head suddenly stopped short, almost wrenching his neck. There, beneath the highway they were all departing posthaste, was a tunnel of some kind. It had a few feet of sand in front of it and a door-sized slab of concrete, but inside it quickly disappeared into darkness—protection, a shelter.

"This way!" he screamed out as he started forward through the rubble toward the opening, about fifty feet off. "This way!" He tried to find them all, standing up on the footrests of the all-terrain. They had all landed, he could see, basically in one piece. Even the tanks had hurtled off the side like overweight mammoths and come down after about forty feet of flight. But suddenly Stone saw even from the fifty yards or so that separated them that one of the Indians had cracked up bad, his three-wheeler coming down smack in the middle of a bad-ass boulder with sharp, poking edges. His brains and guts lay splattered all over it, drenching the rock in red. But the rest of them, although they looked dazed, seemed okay.

Stone searched for some kind of horn on the cross-country vehicle and suddenly found it, slamming his hand down and holding it. That got their attention as angry faces looked up, their still vibrating heads filled with pain from the earsplitting air horn. Stone pointed ahead toward the tunnel with an outstretched arm.

"The tunnel! Now! Move, man, there's no fucking time. Move! Move! Move!" With that he started forward and into the tunnel. He had a feeling the weather was about to get really bad. He saw that the single chunk of concrete that sat in the center of the entrance was barely balanced against another piece to its side. Knowing there wasn't time to play around, Stone accelerated right toward the flat side of the eight-foot-high slab, slamming into it with the left side of the all-terrain. The bike and Stone's head seemed to shake and ring, as if they were slamming around inside the bells of Notre Dame. But the rock moved. Slowly the two-foot-thick square slab of roadway fell over and slammed to the ground with a roar of dust and sand.

Stone coughed and wiped his eyes free of the grit as he started slowly in, not sure of just what was inside. But it was almost clean; the sand from the wind hadn't pushed the outer soil and dust in more than about ten yards or so. It must have been a secondary service road or some goddamn thing that ran under parts of the highway. Off in the dim darkness he could see rusting frames and what looked like a line of the trucks that laid down salt when the snows came. There was enough room for his men—even the tanks. Maybe they were going to get through this damned thing, after all. Stone let himself feel just a glimmer of hope in his heart, an organ that had felt as cold as ice for the last few hours.

He spun the all-terrain around, amazed that the thing even ran, so banged up and bashed in was its entire outer frame, and shot back toward the entrance about ten yards off. The rest of them were tearing toward him now, and Stone came right up to the edge of the tunnel, pulled the all-terrain to the side, and stood up on the leather seat to cheer them on. His heart was beating like a cricket's legs, and Stone knew something was about to happen. Just knew it. Something real bad.

"Come on, come on, you goddamn sons of a bitches," he yelled, waving his hands forward frantically like a cop directing traffic. Behind him on the seat, Stone could hear Excaliber growling under his breath, and he knew the animal sensed it, too—the feeling of something dreadful almost upon them.

One of the Cheyenne came shooting in on his all-terrain, then another. They whizzed by him, and Stone yelled as they flew past.

"Keep going—there's room. Aim your lights so the others can see." They shot on into the innards of the tunnel, switching on their beams so that the wide, curved chamber was illuminated with dancing shadows for hundreds of feet. Another of the Indians tore in, and then one of the tanks, which had to slow down as it lumbered past Stone, sending out a spray of dust from its cranking metal treads. Stone gave the thumbs-up and a thin smile, knowing they could see him on the video scan—if it was still working.

"Damn, we're gonna make it," Stone spat out through

dust-coated lips. But the moment he turned back toward the entrance and his eyes picked out the two roaring shapes— one tank and one three-wheeler, the moment he saw Little Bear's face through the darkness of the two A.M. night, riding for his life with Carla beside him, the entire sky lit up like nothing he had ever seen. The light was absolutely white, like the very face of God, too powerful for the human eye to take. And at the very second that he saw the light of darkness, Stone instinctively flung his hand over his eyes to protect them. Even through the fingers he could see the light—the bones of his hand showing white, like looking at an X ray through his own skin.

"Fuck," Stone said with a groan, not believing this was all happening. But he had little time to get depressed about the situation. For the shock waves, the sound waves, the thousand other waves of the ten-megaton superbomb that had gone off twenty miles away came streaming out over the countryside in every direction like an atomic flood, a waterfall of pure death. There was a roar, as if a train were running over him, and then a curtain of dust and rock seemed to completely fill the opening of the tunnel, and he was flung backward from atop the all-terrain. Stone felt his body slammed down into the concrete, as if the hand of God were pressing him down, squeezing him into the earth. There was a tremendous heat, and then the very earth beneath him seemed to vibrate with such intensity that it felt as if his bones were being shaken free of his body, his brain from out of his skull. And as Martin Stone lay half buried in falling dust and chunks of the cement ceiling, he passed out for the third time in two days.

CHAPTER

TWENTY-TWO

DUST WAS falling everywhere. That was the first thing Stone saw when his eyes opened. The air was filled with a billion specks of spinning dust, and he could barely breathe. Voices yelled out to one another to see if everyone else was still alive. He rose and looked around. Everything was covered with the cement dust. It was like a ghostland, a land where nothing was real. The concrete frame of the tunnel had held, but it had poured down a shit-load of particles and chunks from the shock of the explosion, which had roared through the prairie with an atomic vengeance. Stone could see shapes here and there, some of them moving. He ripped a piece of material from his jacket, which was in tatters now, and wrapped it around his mouth to keep out the dust. That was a little better. Suddenly he heard a whine and saw what looked like a gray turtle crawling along. But as it charged forward and the coating partially blew off, Stone saw that it was the dog, still hobbling on, unstoppable by anything God or man had to offer. Stone grabbed the pitbull and felt tears come to his eyes, so dirty and fucked up did the animal appear. Yet still he was bright-eyed, tail wagging and trusting Stone to lead him through an unfathomably dangerous world.

Yeah, Stone thought with a deep twinge of bitterness as he saw what had been wrought all around him. He had been doing a great job of leading them so far. He ripped another piece of material and made a similar gas mask for the dog. The pitbull tried to shake off the cloth wrapped around its nose and jaws, but Stone slapped it hard on the nose twice. Excaliber looked at him with hurt eyes but stopped trying to dislodge the thing.

Another shape moved, ghostly grit-covered arms and hands reaching up from the roadway. Stone felt a shiver run up and down his spine. It was like a horror movie, like one's worst nightmare. But he resisted the infantile impulse to run and helped the shape to its feet.

"Meyra, you're alive, thank God," Stone said when he saw her face beneath the coating. He hugged the Cheyenne woman close so that a little cloud of the particles lifted from her, puffed off by the air pressure of their bodies meeting. As the roar that still rumbled through the ground slowly ceased and the dust cleared a little, they looked around and saw that they were all okay—those who had made it in, anyway. Stone didn't even want to think about those outside. With the beams of their various lights cutting through the dusty darkness like laser swords Stone walked to the entrance and saw that it was covered with sand, chunks of concrete from the roadway above embedded within like jewels set into a pendant. He poked into the mini-avalanche with a piece of narrow steel rod he saw on the road, and it went in over a yard, still encountering resistance. It would take them forever to dig out. But they had a tank.

"Bring the Bradley up and push her through that shit," Stone told Bull, who headed back up into the tank with his three-man crew. "Slowly, slowly," Stone cautioned him as the tank came forward, the Cheyenne pulling their all-ter-rains off to each side. Bull turned the turret completely around so that the 120-mm was facing backward and set the front of the steel vehicle right up against the side of the collapse. Then he started slowly forward, inch by inch. The tank went into the obstacle like an elephant into a hundred-foot tree. At first the whole surface seemed to push back easily, then the Bradley met more resistance. Bull slowly increased the power so the treads were grinding against the concrete tunnel floor, sending out glowing sparks into the darkness like a hailstorm of fireflies. But slowly the wall slid backward until suddenly with a rush of air and dust the whole thing collapsed in an outward direction, and the tank lumbered through and into the outside world, the deadly world that awaited them.

The rest of them rode their all-terrains up over the yard or so of debris that still covered the opening and headed fifty or sixty feet out onto the prairie. The sky was a throbbing or-ange-green, a sick dead color. Then they all stopped and turned to see what the hand of man had wrought. The mush-room cloud was still rising to the clouds and above, going ten, fifteen miles up. The gargantuan funnel of mega death glowed like a furnace, writhing in dark oranges and reds, as if a beast were caged inside, a killing beast that had been released and now was caged again inside the Day-Glo mushroom-shaped cloud that must have been a good two miles wide. Now that the shock waves and the radiation and every other goddamn thing that a hydrogen warhead puts out when it blows its stack had passed them, it was eerily quiet, without a sound, except for a very deep low-pitched hum, almost subsonic, that seemed to vibrate up from the very earth beneath their feet.

Stone remembered the words of the men who had been responsible for directing the Manhattan Project—the top-se-cret operation that had created the A-bomb—Robert Oppen-heimer, upon witnessing the first test blast. "I am become death, the destroyer of worlds." It was worse than that, Stone thought bitterly to himself as he stared at the grave of mankind, the end of the line for a species that didn't have enough brains to know not to blow its own fucking brains out. The burning cloud was evil; he could feel it laughing within the fires, laughing at all that it consumed. What other creature in the entire universe was so fortunate—it was created by its master, who then fed himself to it to assuage its hunger. What other energy or entity anywhere received such kind and generous treatment?

Stone looked frantically around for the second tank— containing Hartstein, Bo, and three of the other men. He rode forward slowly about fifty yards out from the highway, which was crumbled up into little chunks everywhere and reached a slight turn in the rift. Stone saw instantly that if he'd thought it was bad below, it was a thousand times worse here, where everything had received the full impact of the blast. One of the three-wheelers and the other tank had been right in the path of the waves of radiation that had poured out—unshielded as Stone and the others had been by the wall of concrete and earth that stood between them and the explosion. Little Bear and Carla lay sprawled by their all-terrain—what was left of it, anyway. For the vehicle had been twisted, melted large tires just pieces of bubbling putty. And the bodies . . . Stone could hardly bear to look at the melted human flesh dripping off bone. Eyeballs, teeth, all oozed down floating in a red mush that spread out around the two of them and collected in a pool.

The second Bradley, which had come to within a hundred and fifty feet of making it into the tunnel, was on its side like some toppled beast of the jungle, looking somehow absurd and ridiculous in its death, though it had been powerful and commanding of respect just minutes before. And Stone could see as he walked through the piles of hot sand that gathered at his ankles that there was no one alive inside. Not with the metal on the armor glowing with a dull pulsing red, the entire tank throbbing with an aura of radiation like a thing alive. Not with a foul, oily smoke drifting up from small cracks here and there. Stone prayed that they had died fast in there.

"He's dead," a voice said softly from behind him, and Stone turned slowly, feeling more and more like a zombie, like a psychiatric patient on a heavy dose of Thorazine. It must have been the radiation he had absorbed—they'd had to have taken some—that on top of every other fucking thing he'd been through in the last forty-eight hours. He was overloaded. With everything. Almost with life itself. He felt sick, in the pit of his stomach, the bottom of his soul.

"Yes, I know they're dead," Stone said in a monotone, thinking she meant the recruits who he had led into hell, who lay forever entombed in an atomic crypt with a half-life of two thousand years.

"No, my brother. That's his body over by the edge." She looked down, her eyes bloodshot and wet.

"Are you sure?" Stone asked in a whisper. "They were pretty . . . beat up. Perhaps . . ." He lied knowing full well who they were.

"His earring," she said, holding it out. "It withstood everything, isn't it funny?" She started laughing as she cupped the still shining golden earring shaped like a hawk's feather in her hand. "It's owner is dead, but it shines on. That's good for jewelry advertising. They should really tell everyone that it's atomic bomb–proof—I'm sure they could sell millions." She was laughing hysterically now. Laughing and crying all at once, on the very brink of madness. Stone reached out and slapped her hard across the face, and she glared at him angrily. She lunged forward and tried to strike at him, a clawful of fingernails to the eyes, but he caught her hand in his own at the last second.

"Good, get mad," Stone said, looking her firmly in the eyes, holding her in his grip like a vise. "Because if you mourn, you'll die. The only way forward, through all this, is anger." Stone knew that they couldn't let their armor down for a second—they had been poisoned. He didn't know how much, but he knew they'd need every ounce of the will to live to come through this. And it was worse than that. For already an immense cloud of fallout was building high above them. Stone could see the clouds of dust spiraling like dark galaxies above them, spreading slowly out miles up. Tomorrow they would drop. Tomorrow, and the next day, and the next for a week or two, they would come down in the winds and the rain. And God help those who were caught directly beneath it, who drank water with radioactive particles in them, ate meat, or even breathed it in. They'd have to get the hell out of there—and fast.

"Well, he didn't give his life in vain," Meyra said. Her copper skin had a reddish tinge to it, as did Stone's. "Patton is dead—the madman is dead. The exterminator of my people is dead."

"Yeah, we won," Stone whispered with a look of deep weariness and pain. "But it's still not over, baby. Not by a long shot." He reached out and held her in his arms, there on the edge of nowhere, as he looked off at the burning desolation that spread off in every direction. It was like the smoking ruins of Hiroshima—every cactus, every bush, every tree gone, wiped out as if they'd never existed. Just a flatland of dust and a building dam of fallout above that looked as if it would burst and pour down on them forever. And Stone prayed, as he held her close against him, pressing her breasts against his chest, crushing her flesh as he tried to feel her life energy, tried to feel something beautiful in the midst of this hell. Stone prayed that the madman was in fact dead. That his very atoms were spinning in the twisting mushroom cloud on the horizon. That he was gone. Gone like Little Bear, gone like Bo and Hartstein, gone like all the hundreds, perhaps thousands, that he had caused to die. Gone beyond, beyond, beyond.